JOSEPH MCGEE PRIVATE INVESTIGATOR:
BOOK ELEVEN

I0658078

MCGEE ON TRIAL FOR FIRST DEGREE MURDER

The Greatest Risks of his Life

BY
CARL DOUGLASS

Neurosurgeon Turned Author Writes With Gripping Realism

PUBLICATION
CONSULTANTS
We Believe In The Power Of Authors

PO Box 221974 Anchorage, Alaska 99522-1974
books@publicationconsultants.com, www.publicationconsultants.com

ISBN Number: 978-1-63747-132-6
eBook ISBN Number: 978-1-63747-133-3
ISBN Numbers, Library of Congress Number, Publication Dates,
Publishers Information

Manufactured in the United States of America

DEDICATION

To my seven new great grandchildren

DISCLAIMER

McGee on Trial for First Degree Murder, the 11th Novella of the McGee series is entirely a work of fiction. All characters and the actions and comments by them are the product of the author and do not reflect any real persons or events. The descriptions of known places such as the Tombs came from research and are not based on any real events or experience. This is not a "docu-drama" or strictly accurate lawyers' court presentation; but rather, it is best described as a "writer's court drama". There are considerable author's license segments; real court action is tedious, drawn-out, and repetitive, with all the legal machinations necessary in a real court event or transcript. The author is not an attorney, nor does he claim to be an expert. The fiction is created to move briskly along with the story being told without the tedium of verifying every scintilla, as is necessary in a real court case; such information is frankly boring and unnecessary for this story.

AUTHOR'S THANKS

The author is grateful for his wife and critic, Vera Nielson, and his son, Attorney Karl L. Nielson for help with legal descriptions, definitions, and courtroom procedures. As always, he is grateful to Evan Swensen and his Publication Consultants team for their skill, professionalism, and artistic talent, in achieving the publishing and printing of this and all his other books. Final gratitude is extended for encouragement, advice, and help to produce the best writing possible, to the great authors of Author-Masterminds and the members and contributors of readers&writersbookclub.com.

CONTENTS

PROLOGUE

McGee complied with the request of Congress to address both houses regarding the murders of a sitting Justice of the United States Supreme court and two interns that became a major worldwide murder investigation and dragnet in which he played a key role in the investigation. He said:

"The Chinese have recently arrested a large number of individuals, joined into what is a consortium which functions as a criminal conspiracy. The billionaires charged–and their underlings who carried out the crimes–are all of Chinese extraction, and the People's Republic of China is determined to act sternly and decisively to punish these mega-criminals and to do so with such robust punishments that they will serve as far into the future as anyone can see, as prime bad examples, and hopefully as deterrents. A note of caution, however. The PRC is unpredictable and largely inscrutable. Right now, it appears that there are two Chinas: Hong Kong and Shanghai. The people of Hong Kong are fighting a courageous battle against very long odds. Meanwhile, people in Shanghai have stepped over that threshold and live well under a Faustian bargain with the CCP. Who knows what will come next?"

"In conclusion, we can still trust the honor and efforts at objectivity and in pursuit of the rule of law of the Supreme Court and its future. Thank you for this privilege of speaking. God bless and protect the Supreme Court, and God bless America."

Whether or not there was any connection or some unlikely perverse coincidence, the day following McGee's dramatic speech before Congress, he received a visit from the Chief of Detectives of New York City, David Belle Jordan, with the explosive statement that he—Joseph, Patrick, Aloysius, Michael, John, McGee–was the primary suspect in a first-degree murder. He was taken forthwith to Central Booking the following day. McGee's psychological zenith immediately fell to its nadir.

Chapter One

ARREST

Prior to his involvement in the case of the SCOTUS intern murder case, McGee had gained a reputation as one of the world's premier investigators, whose firm's services were sought by presidents and potentates, billionaires and oligarchs, business magnates, and the movers and shakers of society at all levels. He and his partners in the McGee & Associates Investigations firm—Ivory White and Caitlin O'Brian–made time to pursue such celebrated cases as the victims of a religious cult and an entire class of Catholic orphans. He was fifty-two years old, slim, muscular, and fit, and a handsome, highly eligible, bachelor by any definition. He no longer had any need to work for money, and at times contemplated retirement and doing something else. He never made any headway with such musings.

McGee had decided to take a much-needed week vacation after the SCOTUS intern murders, but Caitlin already had a different and pressing case for three private eyes to accept. It involved an internecine conflict between two African militias—one progressive and the other conservative–vying for control of Eritrea in the Horn of Africa. At stake was renewal of the country's nearly perpetual civil war. The request came from António Guterres, the Secretary-General of the United Nations, with a guarantee of security and payment.

The three partners had scheduled a nine o'clock in-office meeting to decide whether to take on such a volatile assignment in such forbidding terrain. Shortly after they assembled in the conference room, the firm's long-standing secretary, Evelyn Stutz, entered with an ominous interruption:

"McGee, David Belle Jordan, Chief of D's, insists that he has to see you right now."

"Hummh, sure, show him in,"

Jordan was a burly cop's cop who had never learned to smile. He had white hair in a marine cut which had never changed since his hair was coal black, back in the day. He had a craggy, determined, tanned, face etched with worry lines from days outside tramping around following the work of his devoted detectives who thought he was God, even if he was not a saint. He was in his best new uniform in compliance with the commissioner's crackdown on sloppy cop couture. One PP had just come out with a "uniform appearance plan" that ordered every one of the nearly 35,000 New York's finest to "shine their shoes, cover their tattoos, straighten their hats… and buy new pants." There was nothing casual about the man's stern demeanor or the official appearance of his uniform.

McGee and the Chief of D's were well known to each other having worked on cases together for twenty-five-years, although neither man would have identified the other as being "friends".

Jordan's voice was stentorian even when he intended to talk quietly "with his inside voice" as his wife kept reminding him and their three kindergarten age grandchildren.

"McGee, this is the kind of talk that might be better held somewhere in private."

"It's okay, Chief, Ivory and Caitlin know everything there is to know about my affairs. They can stay."

"Suit yourself. Listen, McGee, there's no easy way to say this. I'm here to escort you to Central Booking. You're under arrest for the premedicated murder of one Henry Kendall Lythgoe, President of Local Union No. 295 International Brotherhood of Teamsters and his wife, Mary Margaret O'L. Lythgoe. "You have the right to remain silent. Anything you say can and will be used against you in a court of law. You have the right to an attorney. If you cannot afford an attorney, one will be provided for you. If you decide to answer questions now without an attorney present, you will still have the right to stop answering at any time until you talk to an attorney. Do you understand these rights as I have recited them to you in front of these witnesses, Mr. McGee?"

"Of course, I do."

"Knowing and understanding your rights as I have explained them to you, are you willing to answer my questions without an attorney present?"

"No."

"The stay in Central Booking will be fairly brief. After that I can't say," Belle Geddes said without looking McGee in the eye. "McGee, do I have your promise of complete compliance and safe behavior if I forego placing you in handcuffs for transport?"

"Absolutely."

"And, do I have your permission to deliver you directly to Central Booking downtown and to skip going to the local precinct first?"

"You do, and thank you, Chief."

McGee turned to Caitlin and Ivory, "Call David Rasmussen in LA."

Caitlin was already dialing the law firm of Rasmussen, O'Herligy, Rodriguez, and Applewhite. The partners were all very familiar with and confident in the attorneys from the time they dealt with the murderous polygamist cult of the "Only True Church of Christ" and its criminal conspiracies.

McGee and Chief Belle Jordan did not speak on the way to Central Booking. The Chief of D's traveled with flashing lights the entire time–despite there being no actual emergency. Cops—apparently–did not have to wait in traffic. McGee did get a small smile from watching other motorists pull off to the side of the road thinking they were getting pulled over by the boys-in-blue. Like nothing else in his miserable life at the moment, it was almost laughably funny, particularly to see their relieved faces as the lights went zipping by. McGee appreciated now—like never before–why cops abuse cruiser lights.

McGee concentrated on what needed to be done next because he knew that the stay would not be anything like "brief" as Belle Jordan had characterized it. He spent part of his time filling out an arrest form called his "Pedigree" sheet which was surprisingly thorough about every part of his past and present life.

A person arrested in Brooklyn, Queens, Staten Island, or Manhattan, is put through the criminal justice system. After being arrested, most people are brought to a NYPD Precinct, the first step before ending up in Central Booking at the Manhattan Criminal Courthouse, 100 Centre St, New York. To McGee, it seemed like a favor to skip one odious part of the process. What the Chief of D's was really doing was to keep McGee from being able to contact his private attorney who could assert McGee's right to remain silent and the right for counsel to be present for any lineups before reaching the Tombs.

The lower Manhattan facility, formally known as MDC [Manhattan Detention Complex]–and nicknamed by inmates and New York citizens alike colloquially as "The Tombs"–resembled an Egyptian Mausoleum when it first opened in 1838. It was quickly swamped with inmates, razed; and in 1942, was replaced with a modern Art Deco, E-shaped high-rise structure with recessed entrances and a ziggurat at its peak. Its South Tower— opened in 1983 became the Manhattan House of Detention [still called "The Tombs]. When the free-standing North Tower opened in 1990, the facility morphed into the MDC and assumed "The Tombs" appellation.

When McGee was led into the facility, it consisted of two buildings–the North and South Towers], connected by a bridge over Franklin Street unaffectionately known as the "Bridge of Sighs" after the infamous Venetian bridge where prisoners condemned to be executed where walked to the plaza below to be either hanged or guillotined. Overcrowding throughout the city required the building of a new extension on the block to the north, bounded by Centre, Baxter, Walker, and White Streets. This extension—the fourth iteration of the jail–officially named the Manhattan Detention Complex, houses detainee and sentenced males, most of them undergoing the intake process or facing trial in New York County [Manhattan] as was McGee that dreary day.

McGee's senses were heightened by his anxiety, and he took in every detail of his surroundings as if it were the last day of his life as he knew it. The bulky grey façade of the MDC is clad in a band of reddish-pink concrete bands extending along the building, projecting its verticality. The few windows are narrow horizontal slits in the concrete, recessed and covered with metal bars—no mistaking the intent of the structure. The tower sits on a windowless, granite, two-story, base that serves as the entranceway, houses the few clearly separate retail spaces, and connects the elevated pedestrian bridge to the older south tower.

The structure establishes a clear tripartite division; a smooth granite base with planar horizontal banding, pillow-like red concrete in the middle, along the body engaged vertical columns, and a concrete lattice on top enclosing the roof. The rustication occurs in the middle, along the body of the building, and not at the bottom, suggestion to the soon to be inmates and the population at large that the structure establishes a clear tripartite division; a smooth granite base with planar horizontal banding, pillow-like red concrete in the middle, along the body engaged vertical columns, and a concrete lattice on top enclosing the roof.

The middle block banding has clear rustication [to build or face with usually rough-surfaced masonry blocks having beveled or rebated edges producing pronounced joints as a façade] across the body of the building and not at the bottom. This was done to communicate to the public that the base of the building is infinitely secure through means in addition to the building's forbidding architecture.

The building had multiple obvious sub-levels below the street with "bullpen" jail cells, created to house many inmates at once, along with underground tunnels connecting to the southern building and adjacent courthouse. The tower holds 500 beds, and the south tower 381.

The Tombs serves as Manhattan's Central Booking inlet to hold everyone arrested in the borough before they see a judge. If convicted–or not released on bail–prisoners are then sent to Rikers Island or other upstate prisons where they complete longer sentences. Like McGee, most people in the Tombs have not been convicted of a crime... yet.

CHAPTER TWO

BOOKING AND FELONY ARRAIGNMENT IN THE TOMBS

McGee walked into the dirty pink colored identification room uncertain what he was supposed to do. For starters, he was told that the booking process should take no more than 24 hours. That guarantee was even posted on the walls of each holding cell and every wall in the booking room on a poster explaining WHAT YOU CAN EXPECT during the booking process. As he was about to get his courage up enough to ask politely about that sign, he overheard a conversation between a bored CO and a fellow prisoner who was reassured:

"That 24-hour BS sounds good and all, but we can keep you here as long as we want. You could be here for 94 hours. Stop looking at me as if you thought I was someone who cared. I don't."

A plug-ugly tattooed weight-lifter in CO uniform pointed silently to the left. McGee stood for his mug shot/booking photograph. It was a simple and quick photographic portrait of him from the shoulders up, face straight on and another turned to the side. Photographing of criminals began in the 1840s only a few years after the invention of photography, but it was not until 1888 that French police officer Alphonse Bertillon standardized the process.

The original purpose of the mug shot was to allow law enforcement to have a photographic record of an arrested individual to allow for identification by victims, the public, and investigators. However, McGee knew that entrepreneurs had begun to monetize these public records in a lucrative mug shot publishing industry.

McGee walked towards a line of forlorn looking men silently waiting their turn to identify themselves and to get their numbers: when it was his turn, he was assigned an arrest number—a unique number assigned by the local law enforcement agency to identify a specific arrest of an individual. The arrest number corresponded with the borough in which he was arrested—Manhattan. He said nothing, simply memorized the number, and stood with a soda-cracker expression in his newly placed handcuffs.

"What's the charge?" the portly male African-American clerk asked in a practiced monotone, adding what sounded like McGee was being given a new jail name that cast aspersions on his maternal parentage.

"First degree murder," McGee answered blandly making a huge effort to control his emotions, the tone and cadence of his voice, and his facial expression.

"You innocent, I suppose, SOB?" the nice desk clerk asked politely.

McGee remained silent maintaining his bland soda-cracker expression. The CO laughed uproariously at his own cleverness.

The friendly officer pointed towards his left and said, "Next," [making McGee's name a general reference to an excretory portal].

McGee shuffled to his right until he looked into the plexiglass security window of the second CO, this one a frankly obese woman with short kinky black hair, eyes that were slit-like in her unhealthy fat face. Her expression was unrevealing, and her gaze was a thousand-yard stare almost glazed over with boredom.

McGee felt like he was shaking, and he did not want to appear either anxious, confused, or afraid, despite being all three. He rested his tired hands on the narrow counter.

"Don' you touch nuthin'." [she included his new name]

He removed his hands.

She extracted a paper from her printer, spent a second perusing it, and pushed the document out through the mail slot at the bottom of her window. A second sheet contained information she needed. That she put in his official folder. The information was the OBLS [On Line Booking Sheet] for the OBLS system. He—the arrestee–had provided his pedigree information to the AO [Arresting Officer], in his case, New York Chief of Detectives David Belle Jordan.

As they first walked into the Tombs, the AO had entered the information into the system that assigned the arrest number. This is the first number used to track a new arrestee as he or she is processed through the criminal justice system. The AO had verified that the arrestee did not have any outstanding warrants and that he had checked the various databases to see if there are any issues. That, he had done before he ever came to the offices of McGee & Associates Investigations that morning.

"Don' ax no questions, ya heah?"

She was not interested in any reply; so, he took his own sweet time scrutinizing the new life-altering document. The legalese of the document—entitled a DAT [Desk Appearance Ticket Processing Ruling] was terse in the extreme. There was a simple clear statement that defined when an arrestee could not be granted a DAT:

> "A DAT [Desk Appearance Ticket] is NOT permitted for the following (the charge has to be processed through New York central booking):
> A felony, B felony, C felony, and D felony charges, all sex crimes such as PL 130.25 – Rape in the Third Degree, PL 130.40-Criminal Sexual Act in the Third Degree, absconding crimes such as PL

> 205.10-Escape in the Second Degree, PL 205.17-Absconding from Temporary Release in the Second Degree, PL 205.19-Absconding from a Community Treatment Facility, PL 215.56-Bail Jumping in the Second Degree, and all violent crimes."

He was informed that he could not be given a DAT because of the gravity of the charge against him: an A Felony, viz First-Degree Murder, and that it was potentially a capital crime. An inadvertent chill ran down his spine seeing that written out so starkly. It meant that the NYPD was going to hold him for central booking and immediate arraignment. It clearly meant that he was not going to have a so-called "custodial arrest" which would require spending a mere twenty-four hours in custody.

No, Sir. He was doomed to remain in the fearsome Tombs for an indefinite time he was coming to realize. Due process is irrelevant. The people who go through the booking process have not been convicted of anything. Yet, they are treated like convicted criminals and held in custody. He also learned that many guests of the city had been in custody for extended periods of time. He further learned that many of the same guests had been in custody for several days before they even got to meet with an attorney, contrary to the laws of the city that required meeting with their lawyer and appearing before a judge in the same 24 hour requirement.

The paperwork for many inmates somehow been lost between the time of their arrest and when they were taken to the holding cell where they were supposed to be on a list to meet with a public defender. When they told NYPD officers that they had been there for days and asked the COs to check on their paperwork, they were told to "p... off".

McGee was coming to face the grim reality that he would have to stay because they won't let him leave, simple as that. Would he ever get to see his lawyer? Would he ever be able to learn what had happened, what was going on? He was going to have to suck it up and to spend the next however many hours working his way through various stages of the NYPD's booking process. He had no good idea of what lay ahead or that he had yet to discover more painful—in most cases urine-related—realities of the criminal justice system in New York City.

He was becoming ever more depressed and tired... and afraid. Finding himself in hand-cuffs and waiting to see a judge for an arraignment at some unknown time was becoming an extremely traumatic, life-altering, experience. McGee's heightened psyche added in the complexity and uncertainty coming with COVID-19. He had followed the pandemic on CNN regularly and knew full well that courts and prosecutors' offices were stripped down to the bare essentials in terms of staff, judges, clerks, and even availability. Now his fears ratcheted up to fret over the fact that he was going to be at a higher risk of contracting the virus in a holding cell or a jail like the Tombs and Rikers

Island. He had always considered himself to be a stalwart soul and able to cope, but this was a combination over which he had no control. He still had enough composure to realize his fears and confusion; and more, that he had to gather his wits and prepare for the worst which he was sure was yet to come, COVID-19 pandemic and all.

FINGERPRINTING, the next sign said. McGee had been fingerprinted several times before: when he entered the army to serve in the tail end of the War in Korea, when he was certified as a private investigator in the State of New York, and several times when he performed services for the then DCIA, and now President Sybil Norcroft Daniels. He was familiar with the process and prepared to cooperate fully and quickly. His last fingerprinting had been digital, and the process of the Tombs was the same. McGee was aware that the modern technology, of digital fingerprinting was more accurate and more secure than the traditional ink method. The Tombs was up-to-date with a combination of the X-07 and X-09 locks–electronic combination locks found on most new GSA approved security containers.

"Put ya fingahs on the lighted screen, inmate. Ah'll take all a yer fingerprints on our LiveScan machine," ordered the CLPE [Certified Latent Print Examiner], a designation emblazoned above the right pocket flap of her blouse uniform.

She took electronic impressions of both his complete hands, palms, and each finger, on the lighted LiveScan screen quickly and efficiently.

The fingerprinting secretary completed his form.

"We will make three copies; one is for youse when or if youse evah git outta prison and if youse wants one; the Tombs gits one; and the last one is foah the DOJ and the FBI. Once we ah done we will electronically submit y'all's fingerprints to the DOJ and FBI. Average processin' time is 3-7 business days. That's pleny a time for guys with a rap sheet like yers."

He was resigned to hang on to his sanity despite all and got his next and more fundamental test shortly thereafter when he was taken to his holding cell. The shoving CO did him a service.

"Gimme your sport jacket, [new name in the jail]. You won't last the night lookin' like the uptown privileged elite White guy. Look around, [the other name he was beginning to have to accept]; not many look like you with manicured nails, salon cut hair, and shiny new shoes."

He handed over his navy sport coat and his shoes with an inaudible sigh. In the hallway connecting the roughly five cells was various accumulated garbage of some considerable past vintage–McDonald's bags, a couple of syringes, candy wrappers, plastic grocery sacks, and other crumpled fast food waste.

He had to resign himself to accepting the reality that he would be spending the coming night at least in the holding cell with 20 other people—to use the term loosely. He watched the old vets of the system vie for certain positions in the cell that might prove to be as comfortable as possible. Actually, it was pretty much an impossible task in a room that was 15' X 20' with a concrete floor and wooden benches bolted along each of three walls. As he was pushed into the room, he discovered that the temperature was 90+degrees—a factor that exponentially increased the body odor stench and the scent of urine permeating the crowd, the floors, the walls, and the grimy clothing. For McGee, it was not so much the heat as it was the humanity. Sleep was out of the question.

Guys talked about drugs, booze, women, and bail, in that order. The Blacks–including CO–talked smack with each other calling their listeners forbidden racial epithets with nonchalance. Of interest to McGee, was that none of them cast aspersions at him or disrespected him for being the only Caucasian in the squalid room. He was as sweaty, uncomfortable, and anxious, as the rest of them. The holding room in the Tombs was a great leveling place. Every man and woman there was at the nadir of his/her existence, and there was no point in making it worse for anyone else or for yourself.

McGee did not watch much TV or go to movies with any frequency; so, he had not seen portrayals of the subterranean life in a New York holding cell. He was nauseated from the smell of urine, almost as if it were a mist in the very air. The CO's dragged an unconscious drunk and shoved him through the barred door onto the cell's already putrid floor. He was breathing, but not reactive. McGee watched in horror as an action Goya tableau enfolded. Out of pure meanness, several of the 20 inmates awaiting arraignment began to kick the defenseless old man. They threw boxes of sticky Rice Krispies on him giving him a modified "tarred-and-feathered" look which was a cause for general hilarity in the tight pungent uriniferous room. The old man was covered with fleas which jumped and skittered with each kick. He was spat upon, and urinated on, each contributing to the general comedic atmosphere.

Finally, McGee could not stand it any longer. Despite knowing that he risked real injury and a night of hell, he spoke up.

"Hey, brothers, don't kill the guy. He's just drunk; he hasn't committed a capital crime. Think how it would be if you were beaten and kicked when you were defenseless, or if this was your dad. C'mon, leave him alone."

He expected to be set upon, beaten to the horrible floor and stomped, cursed, disrespected by curses and epithets. But none of that happened. Not so much as a "honkie" hurled at him. That he was White… the only White… seemed to be irrelevant. He was just another miserable guy in hell with the rest of them, and he was making sense.

To his great surprise and relief, the kicking stopped. It was a good thing because the old codger would not be able to survive much more of the stomping; but also, his bowels chose that unfortunate moment to evacuate. If McGee or any other man in the holding cell had thought the smell of urine was terrible, the new collection of odors was logarithmically multiplied. Everyone huddled to walls to get as far away from the source as possible in the confined space. McGee's Good Samaritan urge did not extend to touching or otherwise trying to help the injured drunk.

The show was over, and the long night was closing in. McGee listened to the rudimentary and self-centered conversations around him.

An elderly man with a four-day stubble complained about his ongoing criminal case as he hobbled back and forth on a knee that obviously was in need of being replaced soon.

"Look, Man, I was arrested a month ago in the 14th Street-Union Square Station and charged with petit larceny and possession of stolen property."

"Wuz, youse guilty?"

"Yeah. So, what happened was, Central Bookin' was way overcrowded. I was surprised to be given a DAT and told to come to court twenty days later. You know what that is?"

"Yeah."

"I wasn't arraigned, just kept in limbo. Came back for my twenty-day court appearance, but it got continued… judge sick or something."

"Bummer."

"Yeah, you could say that. Happened again the next court date. Closed because of COVID. Since then, I been suspended from my job because of I have the open criminal case. I can't pay bills, can't eat nothing worthwhile, behind in my rent, nothing."

"Man, you bein' screwed. Must be some law gets you off."

"Don't matter. It's you against them, and I can't do nothing. I can't afford no lawyer, and I can't get me a court appointed attorney until I get the arraignment. I can't get the arraignment because I don't have an attorney."

"Vicious circle, Brother. Like everythin' in the lifes of guys like us. Big bummer."

Two Black men in their early twenties finished their fascinating discourse on the remarkable mammeries of a girl named Millie Sue Oldroyd then settled into a gripe session about life with a felony rap sheet.

"Glad ah don' have two nuthah felonies, else Ah would be up for life in the joint."

"Might's well be. Wit' mah record, can' get no job, can' fin' no decent girl will marry me, even haven' trouble gettin' in with the Crips. Too white. Can' win fo' losin."

An older black man gave his opinion to a younger man, "Lookah' heah bouy, you gotta git Jesus, git saved. Ain't no life wit'out His savin' grace. White world don' give us no choice 'til the Lawd come agin and make everythin' rahgt agin. Ya heah me, Son?"

Nobody slept; so, it was 24 hours of such conversations, punctuated by occasional screams, frequent outbursts of profanity, scatological descriptions, and levels of obscenity the likes of McGee had yet to hear the full extent—apparently–despite his considerable experience with the dregs of humanity.

McGee had been arrested on a Friday, a bad day for anyone held in a holding cell in the Tombs. The justice system got a break from the law requiring arraignment in 24 hours. Because it was a weekend, it would not be his turn for 72 hours. He hoped he would be sane until then… or even alive.

The contents of McGee's new home-away-from-home cell included: a scarred jailhouse toilet with no tank top. The bowl contained what looked and smelled like half a gallon of urine, dozens of vigorously buzzing flies, floor littered with cigarette butts, crumpled papers including torn up DAT cards, and a crumpled partly torn piece of a *Jehovah's Witness Watchtower and Awake!* religious pamphlet, with the words "Enough of this crap" scribbled in an ink marker scrawl.

It could not escape notice that there was also a half-eaten Snickers bar that a rat that somehow lived under the toilet was attempting to eat before McGee stomped his foot to shoo him away. He was not at all tempted to touch anything but the yellowed *LA Times* paper that was temporally substituting for toilet paper. That told him why the toilet had not been flushed in a fairly long time.

Monday morning, just under 48 hours after his having been arrested, his number—along with eight other potential felons–was called out; the barred door was opened; and the nine sighing men were pushed and prodded along to take their places seated behind strong steel mesh deck wire. They were in a place called "New York City's Criminal Court, AR2", the arraignment court. The place was eerily silent.

A female CO called out McGee's number when his turn came and escorted him—still in handcuffs—to a separate private room containing a computer and video setup to meet his counsel. The screen opened up and a distinguished greying gentleman in an obviously custom-made dark suit appeared.

"Hello, Mr. McGee. I am Yitzchak Zalman Teitlemam. I am the lead attorney for the New York branch of the Los Angeles firm of Rasmussen, O'Herligy, Rodriguez, and Apple-white. David Rasmussen asked me to handle your case, if you are agreeable."

The orthodox Jewish man was his only straw to grab, and McGee took no time to answer, "Agree."

"Good, we have very little time. Let us not waste it on idle chatter. You can feel secure here alone with your personal attorney. This room is electronically sealed for the two of us, and the separate locations provide safety from the pandemic virus. I will first give you a very brief discussion of the arraignment process which will also be on zoom—everything in remote locations today and for the duration.

"The process will be remote pretty much like we are doing now. There may be a few junior staff people present, but probably not because of COVID. There will be a few NYPD officers taking care of their end of things. The arraignment then proceeds with the judge and prosecutor being added to the video conference from remote locations. I will be at this same televised remote location to help take care of you and your rights. Do not speak unless spoken to, and more importantly, do not communicate anything unless I give you the nod. Either you or I will be asked to enter a plea of guilty or not guilty. Let me do the talking. The plea will be "not guilty".

"You and I will have a chance to talk in depth later, but for now apply the KISS principle."

"Keep It Simple Stupid," McGee interrupted.

"Just so. At your felony arraignment, the court will inform the–*the* defendant, you–of the substance and details of the charges against you. If things go as usual, defendants receive a copy of the indictment and/or the details of the charges against them. After the court apprises you of all charges, you will then asked how you would like to plead. Bail–if permitted–is set at the felony arraignment today. During the hearing, defendants are allowed to ask for bail or to be released. I will do that for you."

"Courts consider a number of factors in determining how to set bail or whether to release the defendant pending his trial. If the defendant poses a flight risk or if the crime for which the defendant is being charged is violent in nature, a court might remand the defendant to custody. If the court is convinced that remand is necessary, a defendant may request a bail hearing for a future date. I cannot tell you for sure how this is going to go; but, frankly, I think it is going to be remand since the charge is first degree murder. Any questions?"

"No... well, maybe one. Do you care to know that I am innocent?"

"No, but I will want to know every other single thing related to the case that you know, and everything you did on the day of the murder as well as everything you know about the decedent. But that is for another day."

There was a sharp rap on the door.

"Number NYPD 10451-05222022 FEL-M,1 front and center. Arraignment process ready for you. Come PDQ... meanin' NOW!"

The door swung open, and the escort matron entered and beckoned.

"See you in the virtual courtroom, Mr. McGee," Mr. Teitlemam managed as the matron marched the somewhat shaken defendant from the room.

He took his seat in front of the camera and looked straight ahead with a bland facial expression.

"Are you Defendant JPAMJ McGee?" the court clerk asked in here South Bronx accented monotone.

"Yes, Ma'am."

"Do you understand the arraignment process you are about to participate in, Mr. McGee?" the judge [Hon. George Washington Crandell] asked.

"Yes, Your Honor."

"Is your attorney of record present?"

"I am Yitzchak Zalman Teidlemam of the firm of the New York branch of the Los Angeles firm of Rasmussen, O'Herligy, Rodriguez, and Applewhite, member of the New York bar, Your Honor."

"Is your client ready to proceed?"

"He is."

"How about the prosecution?"

"James Hansen, ADA, New York Department of Justice for the prosecution, Your Honor, present and prepared."

Judge Crandell took a moment to read the crime report and arrest record.

Any other felonies or misdemeanors on your client's rap sheet, Mr. Teitlemam?"

"No, Sir."

"Mr. Hansen?"

"Not yet that we can find."

"Plea."

"Not guilty, Your Honor," Mr. Teitlebaum answered crisply.

"We will have to set a court date. Bench or jury, Mr. Teitlemam?"

"Jury."

"Agree," Mr. Hansen?"

"The government agrees."

"Now for the matter of bail. Mr. Teitlebaum?"

"The defense requests ROR, Your Honor. The defendant is a well-known and well-respected member of the community, has a clean record, close ties throughout the community, and presents no flight risk."

"Mr. Hansen?"

"The defendant is charged with a very serious violent crime, has no verifiable alibi, and has many contacts throughout the country and abroad, including many people in the underworld as a result of his wide experience with them in the course of his career. The government requests immediate remand."

"Any rebuttal from the defense?"

"Your honor, my client is willing to surrender his passport and to be placed under monitored house arrest. I give you my personal assurances and that of all members of my firm—even to the point of offering up the funds for a bail bond if need be. We are that certain."

"That is impressive, but I am afraid the government has the law on its side. There would have to be very special circumstances for setting bail in any amount given the serious violence of this felony charge. Bail is denied. However, we can schedule an appeal hearing on the subject of bail one month from today. Adjourned."

Now, JPAMJ McGee had a Rap Sheet [Record of Arrest Prosecution] all his own that would never be expunged, even if he were to be found innocent—a highly unlikely outcome in US federal court, which still retains the death penalty in its prosecutorial armamentarium.

McGee was led back to his temporary new quarters in the Tombs to await transfer to Rikers Island until such time as his trial commenced. No EDA as yet.

CHAPTER THREE

RIKERS ISLAND

At 0600, the following day, McGee was placed in a blaze orange prison jump suit, handcuffed with his wrists behind him, and fitted with wrist and ankle Yoghourds Double Lock Cuffs. Those restraints were attached to a waist chain and thence to ankle cuffs which chaffed the skin and bony protrusions of his ankles. He was escorted by two COs to a line of similarly secured defendants bound by bus for Rikers. The bus was devoid of amenities and had small steel barred windows. The all-male prisoners were escorted onto the bus and placed two-by-two into the simple metal seats without cushions which were bolted to the floor of the bus. The men were shackled together, and the man in the aisle seat had his wrist cuffs further shackled to the floor.

There were three sets of two machine gun armed prison security guards who stood at equal intervals and remained there very intent on the prisoners. McGee made a conscious effort not to talk to anyone on what was supposed to be a 45-minute prison bus ride from the Tombs to Rikers Island in the East River. Rikers is only accessible via the single Rikers Island bridge [officially the Francis R]. The prison took the prisoners to Hazen Street and 19th Avenue in Queens, which is the entrance to Rikers Island.

As the sun was coming up the COs gave each prisoner a sack breakfast/lunch consisting of an unbuttered bologna sandwich, a small bottle of water, and an orange. A few of the inmates managed to peel their oranges, but McGee was not one of the fortunates. He fumbled with the task, hampered by the shackling apparatus and watched it drop to the floor and roll somewhere to the back of the bus out of sight. It was a hungry ride, and part of a long hungry day.

It was a hot trip–no air conditioning. One of the three buses broke down; so, all the inmates had to stop and sit shackled in their hot blaze orange prison garb on the shoulder of the road in the buses and wait for help. It ended up taking five hours, hardly an auspicious beginning to an extraordinarily unpleasant experience.

The bus was bad, but the arrival at Rikers would stick in his mind for a very long time. The double fencing covered in Concertina/Dannertwire and the guard towers [with one officer per tower after two officers were videoed having sex on the windowsill by Rikers' investigators] let him know that he was finally there, and he was not going to leave until they said he could. This was most certainly real. The complex–operated by the New York

City Department of Correction–has a budget of $860 million a year, a staff of 9,000 officers, and 1,500 civilians managing 100,000 admissions per year and an average daily population of 10,000 inmates.

No, it was not a nightmare from which he would awaken in the morning and shortly forget about. It was a feeling of hopelessness, dread, and fear; McGee knew he must put out every physical and psychological effort to try and accept the unacceptable. He still felt like he was in some sort of trance or dream; but before he spoke his first words on Rikers Island, he knew he was not in any kind of dream. He was beginning to sweat.

"*McGee*," he said to himself in his best boyhood brogue, "*me lad, get hold yerself and git on with whatever needs to be done. This is the day ye put on yer long pants and buckle up.*"

His mind cleared, and he came to grips with the first order of business: "*You are going to prison. Seeing all that barbwire and cement takes care of any other notion.*"

His arduous bus ride from Central Booking was quickly forgotten. He had arrived.

In the last mile of the bus ride, one of the onboard guards had said, "Take a look around, a…...s. This is the last look of freedom you guys will see for years."

On the left of the prison entrance to the crowded intake area of the Otis Bantum Correctional Center–one of eight jails on the island, where new admissions are pro-cessed–was an ice cream parlor—to punctuate the poi-gnancy of what was being given up.

He and his prison mates were put in a holding cell along with another load of so-called "fresh" inmates. The holding cell was ridiculously tiny, and McGee was stuffed in there with other inmates, none of whom one would invite to one's house to meet the wife and have dinner: gang members, the mentally ill, homeless people, inmates who are on their way to a maximum security facility to serve upwards of 10+ years—maybe his eventual fate. There was only one toilet inside the cell for the 25 or so newcomers–85% of detainees were pretrial defendants like McGee, either held on bail or remanded in custody– and it had no doors, just a partition. There is no privacy in prison.

There are two long benches inside the cell but not enough for everyone to sit on. Most people stood and some slept on the floor–which was absolutely disgusting. He was ready to deal with the same awful scents he had encountered in the Tombs–everything from urine, feces, and the body odor of those who had not showered for days or weeks. One improvement over the Tombs was that some of the sick, homeless, and disease-ridden home-less men had been required to set aside their free-world lice-ridden clothing—one odor producer a little less. As the system ground slowly towards sorting each man out on that first day, McGee spent of 6+ hours standing inside the holding cell. Sitting or reclining on that foul, filthy, gross, floor would be a final life's effort before giving up and dying for McGee and several of the other incoming pris-oners. One sick old guy told him that the previous week had been much worse due to the COVID. He had been in intake for a week. He said that there were no COs; they were not feeding people; there was no water, no showers, no phone calls. More than a hundred screaming men were crammed into pens for days on end as they waited to be assigned a housing unit that week.

After six hours in the ante-chamber to Hell, McGee was taken to a separate office and processed. His information was entered into the system, and he was given a new address: Inmate Name, ID Number, Hazen Street, East Elmhurst, Queens, New York 11370 for mail. He returned to the holding cell and waited another two hours until a bored CO called out his name—his actual name, not the number he was assigned to be—and he was finally able to leave the holding cell.

Another CO handed him a green cup, a blanket, a short rubber toothbrush, and no-name toothpaste. No razor.

The CO ordered McGee and the twelve other new inmates, "Remove all the clothes you come in with. Do it now, and you don't wanna make me wait. I get grouchy."

Compliance was not uniformly a happy thing, but it was quick.

The CO then handed each man an identical green jumper and orange slippers without any sole padding. The CO did not care what size any of the men usually wore. Whatever the prison had on hand that day was what the newbies were going to wear, period. McGee's slippers were just a tad too large, and he considered himself lucky.

"Youse have the option to put on yer nice new clothes now, or youse can shower before you put on the jumper. Don't never say I didn't ever do nothin' nice for the lotta youse."

McGee opted for the choice to shower first. The showers were open in front of everyone. There was no temperature control for the person showering, and the water temperature was not subject to control by the inmate showering. The water was too hot for any of the new inmates. A few complained, but the COs could not have cared less. McGee made a quick five-minute job of it—a skill he learned in the army.

Once he was neatly dressed in prison attire and had all his materials, the next wait was to be assigned to housing unit. That done, a CO guided the new men to their unit. Like all the other men, McGee was escorted to the EMTC [formerly known as the Correctional Institution for Men] on Hazen Street in East Elmhurst. The EMTC–where most new DOC admissions were being processed and quarantined before they are assigned to a housing area—had become overrun with detainees in violation of city regulations.

The Eric M. Taylor Center has 3 floors and holds a total of 1800+ inmates during regular periods, with each inmate assigned to a specific housing unit. Unfortunately for McGee and everyone else, the units were overfilled; and inmates were being housed two and three to a cell, despite New York Corrections Department rules for only one per cell. The units were divided by floor and number. Assignments for cells changed at the convenience of the system; so, McGee and everyone else was likely to be moved multiple times during their period of incarceration. McGee's semi-permanent place of residence became—after three moves—9 Upper on the 3rd floor, cell number 934.

McGee was escorted to 934 only to find dozens of men had crammed together for days in what would one day become his hut but was now just another temporary holding cell amid the chaos of the pandemic. Filthy floors were sullied with rotten food, maggots, urine, feces, vomitus, and blood. Plastic sheets substituted for blankets, cardboard boxes for beds, and paper bags substituted for toilets. McGee had only thought the stench of the regular holding cells was bad. Because he was a first-timer, he was issued a one-time only pad and blanket. Veterans lying around on the floor glared at him with unabashed avarice.

The CO escorting him growled, "Git a sleeping pad while the gitten' is good. Ya git mah meanin', White Boy?"

"I understand, CO. I'll do it as soon as I lose the cuffs. I am sure you think it has been long enough, and I'm safe enough."

"Since ya'll axed so nice-lak, I'll make a executive decision. Stick ya'll's wrists out; so's, Ah kin git a holdt of the lock."

In three minutes, the wrist, waist, and ankle, cuffs were off McGee's body and hanging from the CO's duty belt. He was a by-the-book, spit-and-polish ex-Navy

Shore Patrolman, who kept his belt and Under Armour Valsetz boots polished to the point of reflecting light. He wore an old timer's Sam Browne style belt–the LytHarvest 10-in-1 Police Duty Utility Belt Rig–with pouches, security guard modular handcuff case, radio pouch, pistol holster, badges, key holder, coms, heavy duty cut-resistant plastic gloves, and light holder.

The belt served as a hook for his holster which held a taser—no guns allowed in the housing areas or the yard. The correctional officer's duty belt served as support for his several sets of heavy gear. The thick, wide, belt helped to distribute and to minimize the weight load of the gear. The CO made an about-face and got out of the bestial environment leaving McGee to fend for himself.

McGee tried not to think about the future, not even as far off as bedtime. His first order of business was to procure a clean sleeping pad… at least somewhat clean. How difficult could that be?

CHAPTER FOUR

PRELIMINARY POLICE INVESTIGATION

Mid-afternoon on the day of the triple homicide of Henry Kendall Lythgoe, President of Local Union No. 295 International Brotherhood of Teamsters, his wife, Mary Margaret O'L. Lythgoe, and their unborn baby girl, the preliminary meeting of the Manhattan Homicide Squad that had caught the Lythgoe case. Their general assignment was to investigate homicides and serious Assault 1 cases that involve firearms, to work with precinct detectives, and to find and contribute additional resources to solve cases. The meeting took place in the 1PP spacious office of Chief of the Bureau of Detectives David Belle Jordan who was going to have overall control.

Manhattan Homicide Bureau's best detective, Kyle Ritchens, D. 1, and his partner, Abigail "Abby" Maartens D. III had the day-to-day responsibility for the hands-on investigation. Chief Jordan insisted on complete media black-out on the part of his select team because of the politically touchy quality of the case. Since this was beginning to look like a forensics evidence case, the Chief of the Forensic Investigations Division, Henry McPherson had two investigators from the CSU [Crime Scene Unit]—Lacy Hicken and Karen Bradshaw–and a civilian criminalist—Omar ibn Muhammad–present in the meeting. They were going to perform work in the police laboratory; and Jordan wanted a tight hand-in-glove relationship with the boots-on-the-ground crew for the entire duration of the case, including the trial when it was ready. The two lead detectives of the gang unit—Creston Y. Jones and Lincoln Browne—were on board because of the obvious gang implications of the Teamsters local chief being the main victim.

The meeting began at two o'clock sharp and did not include amenities like coffee or even water.

Chief Jordan walked around the perimeter of the long conference table and introduced each person present by name, rank, and expertise, as he touched each man or woman on his or her shoulder.

"Get acquainted with each other. Get a code name for this case and for every victim and every copper involved. Communicate with each other and with me only by the burner phones my secretary, Ingrid, is handing out. Put the code names and phone numbers in your phone list and nobody else. All calls on these phones will be monitored regularly; so, no hanky-panky on the lines, no calling anyone else but the people in this room on these phones, and don't call anyone ever about this case on any other phone. That clear?"

There was a quick chorus of "Clear, Boss," from around the room.

"Right now, we don't have an attorney with us, but I will correct that by the end of the day. His job will be to keep us all on the straight and narrow legally. His word–like mine–is law. Any questions or complaints about that?"

Another chorus of "No, Boss."

"All right, then, Kyle and Abby will bring us up to date as of this date and time."

Det. Richens spoke first, "We don't have much more than the obvious at this point. What we know is that three persons are dead, and cause of death was clearly murder: Henry Kendall Lythgoe, President of Local Union No. 295 International Brotherhood of Teamsters, age 52, his wife, Mary Margaret O'L. Lythgoe, age 36, and their unborn baby girl. Let me emphasize, no matter what the legal opinions are about abortion, a child in utero is a human being; and when she dies along with her mother in a murder; it is a double homicide. That is not up for discussion. The time of occurrence of the killings is precise: 1214 hours, as determined by the best witness we have found and the wall clock that stopped at the instant of the explosion.

"This seems to be what went down: a first-time visitor to New York–one Gladys Owens Perkins—was allegedly met in the street by an Italian looking 40ish Caucasian male dressed in a well-fitting dark suit, well-shined shoes, and wearing a felt fedora that matched his suit. He asked Mrs. Perkins if she would do him the kindness of snapping a photo of the two victims, well-known New Yorkers—in the lobby of the Hilton Garden Inn Times Square, 790 Eighth Avenue.

For the purposes of orientation, the hotel is located minutes from Times Square, within easy reach of Central Park, Broadway, the Rockefeller Center, and the Museum of Modern Art. The 50th Street subway station is less than a block away. The Italian guy said he was a paparazzo who was known to the famous Teamsters' boss; so, he could never get close to the guy. He offered to pay her a C-note, but—being a nice housewife from the midwest—she said she would be glad to do him a favor and would not even think about being paid.

"They looked into the hotel lobby from the street, and the "paparazzo" told her exactly where to stand and showed her a file photo of the man and his wife. She commented about the difference in their ages and the man commented that "this is New York; you're not Kansas anymore, Dorothy," which made her laugh. She stood in the lobby dressed in her kind of seedy mid-west farmwife outfit and waited for nearly half an hour until the couple intended for the photograph came walking through the lobby, obviously in something of a hurry.

"That's when it hit the fan. She pointed the camera—actually a coarse looking box thing—saw the man's face through the lens and pulled a trigger-like device which she had been told was just the kind of button used in the special camera. She remembered hearing the sound of a gunshot, being almost knocked backwards off her feet with the surprise of the recoil. She dropped the "camera/box/gun" and did not remember anything else but a huge boom and a brilliant flash of light. The next thing she knew, EMS attendants were lifting her on to a gurney and pushing her into an ambulance. A policewoman accompanied her. Gladys was compos mentis enough to tell the uni what happened right up to the explosion. She knew nothing about an explosion other that there was a boom and a bright light.

"There was most definitely a gunshot. No one saw a shooter; certainly no one identified the camera woman. Ballistics so far says that the shot came from a point about level with Gladys's mid-chest. Her bullet was a soft-nosed .22 which punched an entrance wound the size of a pencil eraser in Mr. Lythgoe, went through and through his left lung and heart, and exited through the mid-upper part of his left thoracic back. The exit hole was big enough to allow a soft ball to pass through with ease. He never knew what hit him.

"Survivors who could act as witnesses reported that within half second after they heard the soft gunshot sound, a horrendous explosion took place. It blew the attractive woman to pieces along with six other people who were within the blast range. Nine murder victims in all by the legal definition of a principal accessory to murder—in this case nine victims overall. Until proved otherwise, the so-called "paparazzo" had prior knowledge of the crime to be committed and did something to encourage or assist the main actor to commit the crime. He is a principle, and the law treats him as if he did all the things the other perp did. We will have to find the guy and to prove that he knew the crime would be committed and did some act or said some word to assist the person to commit the crime; but for the time being he is definitely a person of interest in this investigation.

"For the rest of the findings, we need to hear from my partner, D. III Abigail "Abby" Maartens, and from the spokesperson of the forensics team, Lacy Hicken.

Abby Maartens stood and delivered a crisp, short, and to the point, presentation:

"As near as we can tell, the bomb was carried by the wife of Mr. Lythgoe. The nature of the parcel she carried was almost certainly unknown to her. Forensics found scraps of what was obviously wrapping paper. Presumably, the bomb was wrapped as a gift, most likely for Mrs. Lythgoe to give her husband later in the day. We have a host of possible motives and potential persons of interest. That's the problem for us flatfoots; we have to sort them all out. Seems that nobody liked the Teamsters' boss. He had no friends that one could define as such, and he had a thirty-plus year career of offending almost everyone who crossed his path, from criminal gang bosses, leaders of his own and other unions, and individuals who had the misfortune to encounter the man in bars and restaurants on any of several occasions. We have our work cut out for us."

Lacy Hicken from the CSU [Crime Scene Unit] explained in brief the very preliminary evidence collected:

"Mind you, my fellow investigators, this is almost an off-the-cuff presentation, too early to make much sense of the findings. I will not speculate. We have a few pieces of expensive wrapping paper, with both real silver and gold borders around floral designs on the paper. We surmise that it was a bomb about the size and lethality of two hand grenades elaborately wrapped as a present. It was to be Mr. Lythgoe's birthday tomorrow; so, maybe, the package was a gift for that occasion. The couple were dressed to the nines—him in a new Armani tux, and her in a form-fitting embroidered red silk dress from Lauras Fashion Consultants, located at 135 West 36th Street, Suite, 20, New York. We know that because we found a receipt in what was left of her sequin studded evening bag from Lauras. It was dated yesterday. The woman who attended to her wants said Mrs. Lythgoe was happy and excited about the upcoming surprise party for her husband's birthday and was anxious because she had not yet gotten him a present. The goal for the rest of her day was to find something perfect.

"We found GSW residue on Mrs. Perkins's right hand and sleeve of recent origin. She told us that it was the first time in her life that she had held a gun, and even then, she had no idea that the camera thing *was* a gun. She seemed altogether stricken about what she had done... what she had been a part of.

"The blast radius was about twenty feet, what might be expected from the simultaneous detonation of two military hand grenades. We found shards of shrapnel embedded in the floor, walls, the furniture, and in the sidewalk, outside the hotel. They were consistent with our hand grenade hypothesis, but we cannot say anything about the origin of the explosives at this point. News at eleven," she said and took her seat.

Karen Bradshaw from the CSU spoke from her seat, "Our evidence indicates that the bomb explosion was activated when Mrs. Lythgoe saw her husband drop to the floor with a bleeding hole in his chest. She dropped the package. When it hit the floor, the jolt activated the fairly sensitive trigger in the box. It's not my place to say, really; but this appears very much to be a premeditated, well planned, well executed, murder by persons or persons unknown who were experts, who had probably had prior experience. There is a lot to learn before we can connect the dots."

The next speaker was the hardened thirty-year veteran of the gang unit homicide bureau, Creston Jones.

"We have had a look-see of the crime scene, but none of the gang unit coppers have seen anything quite as clever and elaborate as this. That said, the heads of the Teamsters everywhere are in league with organized crime; it's just too lucrative. Organized crime breeds blackmail, intimidation, and murder, as a way of doing business.

Let me tell you a personal story that is illustrative. When I was eighteen, I applied for a job to work for Union Pacific Railroad trucking. I was living in a "right-to-work" state at the time, and I believed strongly in that philosophy. I was a struggling student and really needed a decent paying job. The boss/supervisor—by law, not allowed to be a member of a union—gave me the forms to complete to become a member of the Teamsters union; so, I could work and receive union pay. I would have to pay union dues, and obey union rules, of course. I told him I was willing to pay the dues, but I did not want it said that I was a union man.

"He said, 'I can't hire you on then. If I did, somebody sometime, would find both our dead bodies in a ditch somewhere. I can't do that to my family.' I couldn't escape that logic either; so, I signed on. The pay was good; the dues were minor; and the job was just a medium hard one. However, I was the only guy on the dock who actually put in a day's work; and I watched the featherbedders lounge around on mattresses in box cars all day. When I was promoted to being a driver, there was a near riot. The featherbedders—a dozen of them—came after me with ax handles. The supervisor picked up two ax handles— one for me and one for him—and we faced the cowards down. No one except the supervisor ever spoke to me again on that job, and I did all the loading, unloading, and driving.

"Taken large, that sort of thing goes on all the time. I'll tell you this: I grew up in Cleveland where the union run by the Cleveland branch of the Mafia is controlled by the Salerno and Aovese family in New York. You can multiply that by hundreds of US cities. Here in New York, the gang unit is going to have its hands full trying to sort out the worst motives, by the worst actors, and who have the flimsiest alibis coupled with the best opportunities. We have to start somewhere; so, I am going to have a little parlay with the Lucchese family maybe *capo di tutti i capi* [boss of bosses], rumored to be Damien Markee, who was once the number one in the BK [Black Knights] and now is rumored to be at least one of the head honchos of the Luccheses. To show you how flagrant the outfit is, we are scheduled to meet in the Marble Palace [Teamsters headquarters in Washington, D.C.] on Louisiana Avenue NW, across a small plaza from the United States Senate.

A forensics lab secretary silently and swiftly hurried into the room and handed CSI Lacy Hicken a formal sealed envelope. Hicken signed for it and quickly tore the envelope open.

"Fingerprint found on the camera/gun," ladies and gentlemen. Guess whose?"

She passed it around the room, and every person's lips made the same smug smile as they saw the report.

Chief Jordan spoke up, for all intents and purposes to get the meeting over with and the investigation underway full speed ahead.

"I am sure you all know it, but I personally arrested a prime suspect, PI McGee, who now resides in Rikers.

Unless you prove me wrong, his association with Damien Markee is the clincher in this case. His fingerprint is the final "smoking gun" finding."

You could have heard a pin drop on the Chief's carpet. Was it really over... that easy?

CHAPTER FIVE

ANOTHER MURDER

McGee grabbed one of the three remaining sleeping mattress pads available and unclaimed. He was lucky to get a new one—reserved for first timers. The light blue cover was extremely thick adding to the heft of the one prize possession he was going to be allowed for some time to come. It was designed so that whatever bodily fluids spill on it can be easily wiped off. The pad is instantly ready to hand to the next guy when you leave, if you leave. No serious cleanup was ever planned. The other cons lying about on the floor without padding looked at McGee with homicidal envy. He was going to have to guard his new treasure and his behind with great attention.

The padding inside the mattress was some sort of synthetic batting. Despite the newness of the mattress, it's tensile strength and inflexible firmness was likely to afford all the comfort of cheap thin carpeting. McGee was not so sure that it would actually be more comfortable than the floor where more than half of the inmates were lying. It was evident that most of his new mates did not have the luxury of residence in an actual cell.

Most of the pads in use by men on the floor were thin on one end. McGee learned a new jailhouse trick when he asked a guy who had one of those. The old con had McGee inspect closely; so, he could see that the pad had been torn open and sewn back together with dental floss.

The oldtimer explained, "Pillows is considered contraband, don't ya know? Do ya remember the last time ya slept without no pillow? Ain't that comfortable, don't ya know? So, Rikers has a lotta rules everyone jist ignore. When ya can't solve yer pillow problem on the black market, ya might stuff in summa yer spare clothes, or with the innards of mattresses like I done, don't ya see?"

McGee saw. He resisted asking whether he could get a nice sharp knife or a pair of Cutco scissors and some good needles at the commissary.

"Watch fer opportunities. Once ya get moved inta yer own house, be on the lookout for yer celly to get a transfer to the hole, or to another hotel, or goes home, quick as ya can, stuff his mattress pad underneatha yours. Then with a double pad—when we call a "custom pillow solution"–ya getta sleep like out in the real world... least 'til the next shakedown when you get a ticket and lose the extra pad and summa yer privileges. Lookit at these guys alayin around; you'll spend mor'en a third of yer life on your prison mattress. It's not like the real world. Here, you'll hate every minute of it."

Thus cheered up, McGee found a place among the bodies and the boxes and settled in for an uncomfortable two days on the filthy floor.

At exactly 11:06 in the morning–sometime after McGee had entered the Tombs in Manhattan–an anonymous 911 call was logged in reporting a dead body being found in the penthouse apartment at 443 Park Avenue South Condominiums—57th and Park Avenue, Midtown Manhattan. The spacious living quarters were located on the top—96th—floor of the slender ["toothpick"], almost all glass building. The building was the most expensive one in Manhattan, and the apartments in the building were only for the mega-rich and best-connected. Because of the location, and the owners—called the CMZ, which included a politically connected billionaire New York real estate developer; Paulo Manifretti, a former lobbyist, political consultant, and lawyer–members of Manhattan's elite homicide unit were called.

Lt. Daniel Eberhardt and Sgt. Emily Conraad caught the assignment and both experienced detectives were unconvinced that this was anything but a crank call.

"Been there, done that," Eberhardt said to his junior partner. "This is the third call to 443 this year. Seems like somebody doesn't like the management and wants to make life unpleasant for them. I can still remember when this was the site of the old Drake Hotel."

"Were the other calls about homicide?"

"One was, the other two were about fires and the sound of screaming. None of 'em came to anything."

"I read in the *Times* that the place has had nothing but trouble since it went up," Conraad said. "It has a reputation for creaking, floods, and design flaws"

"Yeah, but just this morning it went on the market for $169 million."

"Really, pretty soon, I won't be able to find an apartment I can afford," Conraad said…"Oh, that's right, I already can't."

"Okay, Sarge, this is our chance to see how the other half lives."

"0.1% is more like it, Daniel."

He smiled and nodded.

The two world weary detectives took the Geared Traction Elevator at 500 feet per minute and were hardly aware of the incredible speed. It seemed like they just stepped into the elevator, and they were there at the penthouse.

Yellow crime scene tapes closed off the entire 96th floor of the six-bedroom, seven-bathroom, two-powder-room, penthouse apartment. The center of activity was the master bedroom of the light and spacious sky-high Scandinavian design suite. A not-so-subtle copy of the latest *Architectural Digest* was open to the page featuring the apartment. The concept of "swank" in that expensive habitat had a very simple base. The interior design was a cluttered mix of several very different styles–from antique to contemporary to what the detectives considered "early Halloween". Combining such contrasting elements could have resulted in striking upscale haute couture or it could have been an odd mix of colors and cheap IKEA-like furniture design which would be a decorating disaster. The occupants had chosen the latter for their $19,999,999 condo.

"Welcome Daniel and Emily," said the unsmiling head of the CSU crew, Carter Benedict. "We probably won't be here long after you get a look. Hold onto your stomachs, Guys, this is a bad one."

And, it was indeed a 'bad one'.

The master bedroom was full of busy CSU officers clad head-to-toe in white hooded and masked Pro-gard coveralls and black rubber gloves, as much to protect themselves as the sanctity of the scene itself. CSI Benedict led the detectives to the victim lying splayed out on a California king-size bed. The sheets looked as if they had been intentionally sprayed with blood. Blood spray ruined the delicate pink walls, bedside tables, and the thick plush white carpet.

The victim was—or recently had been—a slender thirtyish blond Caucasian female, who now scarcely looked human.

"She was systematically hacked to death with a machete starting at the feet and ending at the vertex of her head. The cuts all bled indicating that she was alive during the entire long drawn-out torture. The hacking was frenzied—witness the wide distribution of blood and spatter. She had a beautiful model's face before all this; take a look at the photo on the left side of the bed. This is text-book overkill," Benedict said unnecessarily.

"Does she have a name yet?" Eberhardt asked.

"She does. It's Madeleine Noémie Toussaint."

"Frenchie?"

"Yeah."

"Married?"

"Not sure. Nobody in the hotel seems to know, but maybe they are all part of the 443 Park Avenue Omerta Society of Central Midtown Manhattan. No ring on the fourth finger, left hand, though."

"Somebody really hated this girl, or the killer was crazy as a hoot owl," Lt. Eberhardt said.

"Or both," said Sgt. Conraad.

"Or wanted to send a message," observed Benedict with a depressed shrug.

"Glad this isn't my first case. Makes me want to puke," Emily said, teeth clenched.

"I hate to sound stupid, Carter; but what is the cause of death?"

"It would be easy to write it off as exsanguination, but we really won't know until we get her on the table. We could find deep stab wounds from a different weapon, who knows?"

"Do you have the murder weapon?" Eberhardt asked.

"We do, but we can do you one better. We have about the clearest set of fingerprints you ever saw. They are only on the handle of the machete. Have to be the killer's. It's interesting that there are no other fingerprints in the apartment from our unsub."

"Let's put a lights and sirens rush on them, Carter. We have to find this guy before all five boroughs have a panic."

"Way ahead of you, Daniel. This guy has to be put in custody PDQ before we have a bunch of vigilantes roaming the streets assassinating every crazy they find. You guys have your work cut out for you."

CHAPTER SIX

MCGEE'S ASSOCIATES AND WELL-CONNECTED FRIENDS ENTER THE FRAY

C aitlin O'Brian and Ivory White began their involvement in McGee's legal difficulties within minutes of his having been taken away from their meeting by the Chief of D's. Caitlyn contacted David Rasmussen of the Los Angeles firm of Rasmussen, O'Herligy, Rodriguez, and Apple-white, in LA who assigned the task of defending McGee to Yitzchak Zalman Teitleman, the lead attorney for the New York branch of the firm. Her next call was to her old friend from her time as an NYPD homicide detective and the only one she truly trusted in the NYPD—Detective Sergeant Emily Conraad.

"Em," she said, "this is Caitlin. I need your help."

"Never one to waste time on idle chit-chat, are you? And, I am fine, thanks, just made sergeant, in case anyone cared. I am working my butt off. How's the family? Mine's fine. No, I haven't had time to get married. You?"

"I'm sorry Em. I have no real excuse for not keeping up with you, but I have been involved in some real hairy cases. More than that, I was kind of afraid that it might hurt your career if you were seen with me or if we had texting, emailing, or telephone, records between us. You know how it was when I had to leave. I was considered to be poison. I had violated the "old-boy" system. Let me ask you, have things really changed? Are men given a pass when they do something gross, like in my case. Yes, I slugged him; but I was provoked. You know that, right?"

"Of course, I do, Caitlin. I was just bustin' your chops a little. I miss you. Anyway, I want us to have some din-din sometime and catch up. Right now, though, what can I do to help you?"

"Look, Em, my partner, McGee, is a good guy; and he is in the Tombs, or probably over to Rikers by now on a murder rap. I am at a complete loss about where the charge came from. He is supposed to have murdered some Teamsters big shot and his wife, Henry Kendall Lythgoe, President of Local Union No. 295 International Brotherhood of Teamsters and his wife, Mary Margaret O'L. Lythgoe to be precise. The chief of D's personally became McGee's AO, as much as told us it was an open and shut case. His bid was going to be all day and night at best or more likely, the "big bitch". None of us ever even heard of this Lythgoe guy or his wife, and we have not been able to get enough info to do some digging on our own. I need your help on that, Em."

"Belle Gedes must have some pretty damning evidence to have even suggested life without the possibility of parole and even getting the needle. He's usually pretty close mouthed about cases and keeps his opinions to himself. I'll nose around a little and get back to you, Caitlin. How about dinner at the Kong Sikh Tong Café on Bayard in China Town? It's a good cop joint, and if we go early—like about five like the senior citizens—we should be able to get a seat. Whatta ya say?"

"Sounds great, Em. It's a date then. Thanks."

At dinner in the noisy crowded authentic Hong Kong food restaurant three days later, Emily told Caitlin about the second murder and about the fingerprints being positive implicating McGee.

"Look, Caitlin, courts only require enough to have 8 to 12 characteristics in common; and in both cases, McGee's prints had a perfect 16."

"Perfect, Em? I don't remember ever seeing a perfect print, let alone two sets in different crime scenes. It's gotta make you wonder. It kinda smells like the Copenhagen fish market, if you ask me."

"Enough business, Caitlin. Don't shoot the messenger. Let's enjoy the food and the company tonight. I'll keep you in the loop, but it has to be on the DL. I think you need to try the Hong Kong style milk tea, and the spam and egg noodles come with cabbage. Doesn't sound like much, but I like it. The pineapple bun is so-o good… has a cold piece of butter in the middle while the outside is warmed."

Caitlin hated to tell Ivory what she had learned from Sgt. Conraad. Who knew when they would be able to see McGee in Rikers?

Ivory needed four days to get to talk to McGee's gangster pal, Damien Markee, whose two daughters the investigators had saved from kidnappers a couple of years ago. McGee had played poker with him at Damien's club every Friday night for several years. Damien was a smooth operator by all outward appearances, nothing like one would expect of the boss of the Black Knights [BK] gang and a multimillionaire in large part from McGee and Ivory's help over the years. Ivory White had been a lieutenant in the BK for several years until he saw too many young black men die in "the line of duty". McGee had given him a way up and out to the legit world.

The appointment was at three in the afternoon in the BK headquarters at the benign sounding East Harlem Men's Club on 133rd Street in East Harlem. The club was not a place that drew attention from idle passers-by. The neon sign was missing some letters; so, it read –st Harle- Men's Cl-b, Inc. The front façade could have been designed by Lucky Luciano back in the thirties, and the interior had a sawdust and oyster shell floor nearly permanently. The tables and chairs were a mismatched assortment which had not been upgraded since the sixties. Gave the place "character", Damien told anyone who asked. It was dark enough inside that it took Ivory a full two minutes for his eyes to adjust to the dim light. He was not even able to see the skinny girl working the pole in what passed for something of a dance until he came within fifteen feet of her.

Ivory was ushered into Damien's backroom office by his "secretary" a middle-aged man with muscles on his muscles. He patted Ivory down carefully and fully, and followed him into Damien's office.

The handsome, well groomed, and expensively dressed, thirty-five-year-old leader stood up from his swivel chair behind his cluttered dark antique wood desk and walked to where Ivory was standing and shook his hand warmly.

"Ivory, my friend, I can't tell you how glad I am to see you. I've spent some time in stir, and it wasn't all that bad. But Mexican jails and prisons are like you died and went to hell prematurely. You've got some great friends, I have to say. When I got done reading about the crap the Mexican president and his police did, I thought about reapplying for my former choir boy position. The pay's no good, but the company's about the best around."

They both laughed.

"Something to drink, Ivory?"

"No thanks, Damien. During my vacay in Mexico, I saw so much liquor and drug abuse that I swore off the stuff. I have to say that it's the best I've ever felt."

"Maybe I should join the Ivory White Temperance Society. I'm busy today, I'll have to put it off until tomorrow."

He said it with a friendly grin.

"Enough nonsense. I heard McGee got jammed up. Any real evidence against him?"

"Your guess is as good as mine, Damien. We can't get anything out of our usual sources, the cops, or the hotel people. We're dealing with a deaf-mute and blind society. That's why I'm here. Anything on the down-under network that might give us a lead?"

"Nothing very useful. I have friends on both sides of the opinion poll about the vic–Henry Kendall Lythgoe, President of Local Teamsters and his wife, Mary Margaret O'L. Lythgoe. Everybody agrees that the man was as mean as a black widow spider. His supporters liked that about him; he was their spider. His enemies—which are many—don't trust him, don't like his tactics, and envy his success. Rumor has it that the man is—or was–one of the richest crooks in the five boroughs, and that's going some.

Rumor has it that his nice family friends, the Luccheses are getting ready to go to the mattresses with the Genoveses over who controls gambling in the five boroughs and Chicago. Lotta bad blood there. Ever since "The Oddfather", Vincent "The Chin" Gigante, died, most mafiosos recognize Don Guillermo "Barney" Trafficante as the current boss of the organization. Otto "Six-Fingers" Castellammarese is his number two. He accused Lythgoe in public of raping his—Castellammareser's—granddaughter and that the Luccheses were protecting Lythgoe."

"I heard you were the boss of the Luccheses, my friend."

"Not a chance, Ivory. I'm not even the acting underboss."

"Think Trafficante killed the Lythgoes, Damien?"

"Himself, no. But he has access to multiple hitmen and women from all over the world. The cleverness of the hit makes you think of him. He's got a cool head. If this had been a crime of passion, like, say lots of bullets or stabbings, I would rule him out. For one thing, it would probably be hard to find a motive for such a crime. For the Lythgoes, I wouldn't rule him out."

"Just for the record, could any of the Black Knights have had a motive or have been needing extra cash?"

"I know you need to dot all the i's and cross the t's, but trust me; we are too small to have enemies like that. There's nothing for us to gain."

"Except maybe fomenting a gangster war and picking up the pieces when it ends."

"Not even that, Ivory. None of that money or power is worth anything to dead guys. We stay out of it and far away from it. And no, I don't want you questioning my guys. It would be insulting. You and I go way back, my friend. You, McGee, Caitlin, and I, trust each other with good reason. I trusted you with my two daughters; you can trust me for this piece of truth."

CHAPTER SEVEN

DETECTIVES MEET THE PROSECUTORS

Even before McGee had been granted the privilege of having his own "Hole-in-the-Wall" as the long-term cons liked to call their cells, the two sets of fingerprints found on the two recent homicide victims were rushed through the NYPD Criminal Records Section, FBI IACP National Bureau of Criminal Identification system, and INTERPOL's AFIS. INTERPOL runs an international fingerprint database known as the automatic fingerprint identification system. The AFIS contains more than 220,000 fingerprint records and more than 17,000 crime scene marks. McGee's prints were very recent; there had been considerable attention to his prints; and they were very clear and complete. As a result, the prints found at the two separate crime scenes were near the top of the list in each system. The fingerprint evidence was considered so blatant that all other suspects were shunted to the side, and JPAMJ McGee assumed great prominence in the attentions of the NYPD, the office of the US Attorney for the Southern District of New York, and the New York County District Attorney's Office–also known as the Manhattan District Attorney—and Yitzchak Zalman Teitlemam, McGee's lawyer.

That information had not been released to the press yet, but the cops and attorneys involved knew they were not going to be able to keep it out of the tabloids for long. The two branches of the prosecutorial system considered the McGee case to be pressing enough to have a formal strategy session on the third day after the Lythgoe murders and one day after the Madeleine Noémie Toussaint killing. Lt. Daniel Eberhardt and Sgt. Emily Conraad–who were the first detectives on the scene–logically claimed the rights to head up the investigation. Logic was not of consequence. One PP assigned the case to the task force, led by Kyle Ritchens, D. 1, and his partner, Abigail "Abby" Maartens D. III thereby dealing with the Lythgoe and Toussaint murders on the presumption that they were probably related.

Lt. Eberhardt growled, "Should be our case, Kyle."

"One PP assigned us, Daniel. Who am I to argue with the left corner office of One PP?"

Daniel ground his teeth but knew nothing good could come from an argument with the task force or certainly with the 14th floor.

"Look, it's not fair. At least keep the two of us on the task force. This is a great case. You know it. No reason all of us can't get a little something from being involved. Whadda you say, Kyle?"

Ritchens did not need trouble at this point; so, he said, "I'll do my best for you and Emily, Daniel. Don't get your hopes up too high. Be a bit patient. I'll get back to you when I know something."

Eberhardt knew that was the best he was going to get. Ritchens was a decent sort of guy; so, he let it slide.

The pressure was on; so, the tension was obvious in the large old office in the 1 Saint Andrews Plaza [Silvio I. Mollo Federal] Building, New York. The Office is at the forefront of many important areas of criminal law enforcement, including terrorism, white collar and cyber-crime, mortgage fraud, public corruption, gang violence, organized crime, international narcotics trafficking, and civil rights violations. Murders and other crimes associated with the day-to-day cases handled by United States District Court for the Southern District of New York are automatically handed off to SDNY at the discretion of the police commissioner.

The cops and attorneys seated around the highly polished oval table were heatedly discussing the avenues of approach to the investigation. The two detectives did not care about the cost, but they did care about the amount of work—especially paperwork—that would be generated by widening the scope to other possible perpetrators besides the obvious—JPAMJ McGee. The detail-oriented attorneys feared that they would fail to round up other accessories before and after the fact or interested parties. They were all reluctant to let things get of hand by going after the mafia.

They all remembered the decades long Gotti case and the Mafia Commission Trial—formally, *United States v. Anthony Salerno, et al* which took almost a full year for the trial alone. The US attorneys involved did not care about the cost either since Uncle Sugar was footing the bill. However, the senior attorney, Rudolph Pasolini, knew his career would tank if they got mired down in lengthy and costly avenues of investigation. He personally could not afford to get far afield legally since this was a simple murder case at its core; a few murders–nine, to be exact–an obviously guilty defendant, and plenty of real and actual—instead of circumstantial evidence. All they lacked was a smoking gun.

NYPD Lead task force Detective First Class Kyle Ritchens, and his partner, Abigail "Abby" Maartens D. III were already dealing with the Lythgoe and Toussaint murders on the presumption that they were somehow related, spoke first. They worked in tandem to present brief description [the "Dick and Jane" version] of the case of New York v. JPAMJ McGee:

"This is a quadruple homicide. The victims are: Henry Kendall Lythgoe, President of Local Union No. 295 International Brotherhood of Teamsters, age 52, his wife, Mary Margaret O'L. Lythgoe, age 36, and their unborn baby girl. Method of killing gun and bomb. At a second location, there was a single victim, Madeleine

Noémie Toussaint, age 32. Method of killing, hacking by a machete. All victims were Caucasians.

Crime scenes.

1. Lythgoe scene: lobby of the Hilton Garden Inn Times Square, 790 Eighth Avenue, Manhattan.

2. Toussaint scene: Master bedroom of 96th floor penthouse suite of 443 Park Avenue Condominiums, Manhattan.

Motive or motives: unclear at this preliminary stage and remain under investigation

Pertinent evidence: at each crime scene evidence of the weapons was found; and in each instance, very clear 16 friction-ridge fingerprint evidence was found implicating Joseph Patrick Aloysius Michael John McGee, a senior executive of McGee Private Investigations, Inc. and no one else. The fingerprint in the Lythgoe crime scene was found on a faux camera box which served as an improvised gun. In the Toussaint scene, the print was found within the victim's blood on the handle of the machete which has been conclusively determined to be the murder weapon.

Witnesses: Gladys Owens Perkins, tourist from Kansas City, Kansas.

And there ended the NYPD involvement in the case because it became federal. The case became federal because of an arcane bit of US law. The Historic Sites Act of 1935 declared "a national policy to preserve for public use historic sites, buildings, and objects of national significance for the inspiration and benefit of the people of the United States." It authorized the Secretary of the Interior to obtain information, survey, conduct research, maintain, and preserve sites with archeological significance. The NHPA, Section 1: authorizes the expansion and maintenance of the National Register of Historic Places, the official federal listing of "districts, sites, buildings, structures, and objects significant in American history, *architecture*, archeology, *engineering*, and culture."

Section 462 enumerates a wide range of powers and responsibilities given to the National Park Service and the Secretary of the Interior, including codifying and institutionalizing the Historic American Buildings Survey, authorization to survey significant sites and buildings (which became the National Historic Landmarks program), and authorization to conduct preservation. (c) … that *represent the work of a master, or that possess high artistic values, or that represent a significant and distinguishable entity…* 443 Park Avenue South Condominiums—57th and Park Avenue, Midtown Manhattan fit the definition conveniently.

Ostensibly, for that reason, the US Federal Government elected to take over the case. There may have been a bearing from the fact that there appeared to be a likelihood of organized crime involvement, and it was another opportunity to take advantage of a small crack in the gang-world's power base.

The Investigation:
Federal District Court Judge Hyman Rotweillin was appointed by the DOJ to be in charge of the legal case. He

was a hanging judge; the death penalty was still retained in the federal system; and he would be happy to keep up his 96% conviction rate with McGee going down alone. Taking down some mafioso in addition would be icing on the cake for him but not a major goal. He was nearing retirement and did not need the entanglement of a messy case. He was going to push the attorneys toward quick and efficient justice.

Officers of the Court:

District Judge Hon. Hyman Rotweillin

Attorney(s) for the prosecution: US Attorney SDNY Attorney Milton Weilenbach and Deputy Attorney General Franklin Caruthers.

Attorney of record for the defense: Yitzchak Zalman Teitlemam of the firm of the New York branch of the Los Angeles firm of Rasmussen, O'Herligy, Rodriguez, and Applewhite, member of the New York bar.

Law Enforcement: FBI-SAC William Richard Granthem, FBI Office, 26 Federal Plaza, New York, New York; Cooperating local law enforcement–NYPD-Chief of Detectives of New York City, David Belle Jordan, Task Force- Kyle Ritchens, Detective First Grade, D. III Abigail "Abby" Maartens, and Forensics- CSI Lacy Hicken, Civilian criminalist—Omar ibn Muhammad, and Gang Unit Detectives—Lt. Creston Y. Jones and Lincoln Browne D.I."

In the interest of brevity, Deputy Attorney General Franklin Caruthers and FBI-SAC William Richard

Granthem presented discussions of the crimes, investigations, and status of legal proceedings.

SAC Granthem: "All politics, preferences, and current evidence aside, it is the long-standing mission of the US Federal Bureau of Investigation to seek out the truth. That could not be more important anywhere than in this case. A man's life is at stake here. A rush to judgment on the basis of a lack of motive, inadequate information on the alleged suspect's whereabouts at the times of the two sets of murders is unclear at best, and the FBI fingerprints experts are dubious about such clear and simple fingerprint evidence. We should be so lucky all the time.

So, the FBI will proceed with caution to prepare a clear dossier on Mr. McGee and will have as clear a picture of his activities on the days in question as is possible. It is probable that the bureau will be required to testify as to evidence in open court, and we are strongly averse to having a clever defense attorney upstage us with heretofore unknown exculpatory evidence."

Dep. Attorney General Caruthers: We at the SDNY are in partial agreement with the SAC. However, we are confident in the work of the NYPD thus far and will proceed with plans for a federal criminal trial to take place in somewhere around three months, using the convincing evidence at hand, unless further investigation reveals something new or striking coming out of the work of our investigators or from the defense. My observation to the SAC is that sometimes the perpetrator is just plain guilty, often plain stupid; and a guilty verdict is clear and simple for the jury of his peers. That said, we all have a lot of work to do before now and August."

Caitlin O'Brian showed her cred-pack to the door-man and then to the assistant manager of the 443 Park Avenue South Condominiums building and was pleasantly surprised when they were both cooperative, even friendly. Apparently, the powers that be—CMZ and the day-to-day management—thought it prudent to appear to be coop-erative with law enforcement, even down to private eyes. She took note of the bread-basket sized bronze placque on the front door: NATIONAL HISTORICAL BUILDING.

"What can I do you for, Ms. O'Brian?" asked the assistant manager, Charles Milwright, in his best affected Chelsea Avenue manner and accent. Chelsea is one of NYC›s quintessential gay neighborhoods located on Manhattan's west side, from 14th to 28th Streets between Sixth Avenue and the Hudson River.

"My investigation is about the victim in the recent murder in your penthouse. We're not really interested in your condos and will pretty much leave the building out of our reports if we can find out all there is to know about Ms. Toussaint."

Milwright was a life-long New Yorker and seldom surprised by anything he saw or heard in Gotham. How-ever, even by New York standards, word had gotten out about the looker in the penthouse with a velocity that must have set a speed record. She had seemed so reclusive up to now.

"What sort of info do you need to know? Most of our owners value their privacy even more than their money," he exaggerated.

"Oh, we're not looking to do any kind of exposé. Our sole interest is in the victim and what–if any relation–she had to the alleged killer, McGee. Or maybe if she kept company with gangsters, shady billionaires, or even shadier politicos. Our people are willing to pay the costs of any investigation you do, or to which you can direct us."

"What kind of fees are you suggesting? This is a pretty closed society here, and anything I get will require greasing a lot of expensive palms, is my guess."

"Let's talk about what *you* think is reasonable and fair."

It took almost an hour of negotiation between Caitlin and Charles before she was convinced that he had the information she needed, and he was sure his baksheesh request was as high as she would go. It was all done in polite euphemisms and with a fine theatrical performance by Caitlin, who had to demand of herself that she would not roll her eyes or tell the jerk what she thought of him.

It was another two hours of questioning and digging deep to get at the truth that mattered.

"So, my friend, let's take one more look at these photos. Tell me if the lovely Ms. Toussaint was visited with some regularity by any of these men."

She showed him her photo array of the city's richest mafiosos, top floor NYPD officers, and political movers and shakers. He tried a little maneuvering for more palm greasing before he would give out that information to Caitlin who lost her poker face when she worked to get that bit of gossip. Her trump card was that she had not yet handed over any of the cash she had brought from the office to gain leverage.

"Caitlin, I gotta be straight with you. If it ever got out that I fingered any one of these guys, I would be out of a job, have no references; so, no career, and probably have to learn to walk again, if you get my meaning."

"And just maybe a green poultice would help, that it, Charles?"

He gave her a steely look, admitting that the jig was up; and he wanted more sweetener to loosen his lips. He even gave her a full-toothed, self-satisfied, Cheshire Cat smile, presuming that he had her over a barrel.

Caitlin's patience had worn thin. She smiled seductively and gave him a lightning fast double left tap and a stiff right bolo punch which caught him by surprise and decked the dandy like a pile-driver had hit him. She waited until he came around, then returned his Cheshire Cat smile.

"Charlie, old pal. I hold in my hand ten grand. I can make it twelve, but I will have my info. Failure can make me a PMS monster. Following?"

"Yeah, you don't have to get so testy. Let me see the pix again. I'll see what I can remember."

"Good plan."

He picked out three photos: a gangster, a deputy chief in the commissioner's office, and the Director of Special Enforcement Lawsuit Against Short-term Illegal Rental Operations. The deputy chief had a record of three unwanted touching and harassments, and sexual coercion, and one for brandishing a knife at a woman who protested. The charges were swept under the rug by the PBA [Police Benevolent Association of the City of New York].

The Director of the so-called action against rental operation malfeasance had been milking the system for months. It was a standing joke in the department. To ensure against another sucker punch, Charles threw in the tidbit that the Toussaint woman was skillful at pillow talk and was not above skimming a little from the operations she learned about. He thought maybe she had loose lips as well.

Caitlin underlined the names by the photos: Deputy Chief Lance N. Devereaux, and Director Elroy X. Jackson. She made a mental note to keep those names in mind.

Chapter Eight

McGee gets a
Cell and a Shower

Five days after entering the New York jail system, McGee finally got his own cell—9 Upper on the 3rd floor, cell No. 934–actually one he was to share with another man. His cellie was an intelligent, well-educated, tall, fit, Black, man who was very interested in McGee and everything about him as soon as they met. Because McGee was the first to arrive in the cell, he got the choice of having the lower bunk. Jacob Washington Hartwell, the cellie, was affable and agreeable about the arrangement. He was a Vietnam veteran, well-read, wore prescription glasses, and offered to teach McGee chess. They exchanged names, John Creddlman and McGee. He seemed to know everything McGee needed to know about Rikers prison life and how to keep safe. He explained about prison society—who was the boss, who were his lieutenants, and how gangs divided up the cons by race and gang affiliation. McGee got to ask pertinent questions.

His first questions to his new friend were, "Is it safe to take a shower? How can I stay safe in the shower?"

"Those are good first questions, Bro. It's safe if you go when there are ten or more guys in the showers to act as witnesses. No showering alone or at night."

"What do I do about the gangs and the racial divisions."

"You will never have anything to do with the Blacks or their gangs, or the Latinos either; they won't let you in. That leaves the racist skinhead White gangs. They'll tell you that you won't make it if you don't get affiliated with the White supremacists like the ABs [Aryan Brotherhood, The Brand, Alice Baker, or One-Two], Order of the Blood [a criminal organization controlled by the Aryan Brotherhood], Aryan Nation, Aryan Brotherhood of Texas, Brotherwoods, KKK [Grand Knights of the Ku Klux Klan], 211 Group, Militia of Montana, Peckerwood gangs [including the Nazi Lowriders and Public Enemy No. 1], Hells Angels, American Mafia, Wonderland Gang of drug dealers, Soldiers of Aryan Culture, the Dirty White Boys, or the 1488s.

"It's your choice, just make it soon."

The advice "don't trust anyone", rang in his mind every time he encountered anyone. Only Whites even looked his way, and several nodded or smiled at him. Four different men engaged him in one-way conversations. Their physiques were about the same, large, approaching being muscle bound, bearded, all short haired with military cuts, tanned white skin and tattoos on most of their exposed skin. McGee was fairly sure that he could differentiate the several gang members by their identifying tattoos: Popular tattoos among AB members included a shamrock inscribed with the number "666", swastikas, the abbreviation A.B., the numbers 1 and 2 [standing for AB], and double lightning bolts, which stand for Hitler's SS. New members were branded with a tattoo, following the procedure in a prison novel popular among inmates. The image was either a green shamrock—"the rock"—and the letters AB, or the number 666. That was "The Brand" and having the brand, meant the inmate belonged to Aryan Brotherhood.

The 1488s used Nazi-derived symbols to identify themselves and their affiliation with the gang, including a 1488 "patch" tattoo which depicted an Iron Cross superimposed over a swastika. The tattoo can only be worn by "made" members who generally gained full membership by committing acts of violence on behalf of the gang. Kluckers had a variant of the first Ku Klux Klan tattoo that was used in the early 1920s. Incorporation of a noose was the most significant symbol, representing the large number of lynchings of blacks that took place in the early part of the last century. The Confederate flag formed the backdrop. The tattoo was popular with the KKK and Aryan Nation convicts. Peckerwoods [Woodpile] stood out from other White supremacists by having the term peckerwood in their tattoos represented by various woodpecker images, sometimes in conjunction with other hate symbols. It was also common for gang members to use the word itself for a tattoo, or its common shortened version, "Wood," or "100% Wood."

Teardrops were placed in various places, most of them on the lower eyelids. The most widely accepted meaning of the teardrop is the wearer has killed someone. The teardrop can also mean that the wearer is mourning the loss of a family member. A clear teardrop can mean that the wearer has committed an attempted murder, or alternatively, that a close friend or family member was killed; and the wearer is seeking revenge. A Clock with No Hands was one of the most obvious and transparent tattoo among the Peckerwoods meaning 'doing time' and was representative of a long prison sentence. Many prisoners with long sentences view time as somewhat meaningless, which is what this tattoo represents. *Schutzstaffel* lightening bolt images were also favorites to honor the violent Nazi paramilitary ranks.

American mafia prison gang tattoos include a mix of symbols in ink. A cobweb on the back indicates a long term; the 3 dots tattoo–worn either on the hand or near the eye–is another highly recognizable prison tattoo representing. the phrase "*Mi Vida Loca*" or "My Crazy Life." The dots tattoo can be found on many Mafia inmates which often carry religious meaning, representing the Holy Trinity with the Catholic mafiosos. They also like EWMN [Evil, Wicked, Mean, Nasty]. These tattoos are frequently inked in prison and are commonly placed across the inmates' knuckles of their dominant hand; so, it is the last thing someone sees before they get knocked out. The tattoo "72" means that if you see it touch your hands, i.e. by meeting this person, you just got dealt the worst possible hand by them [a reference to Texas Hold'em poker].

With all that prison info tucked away in his mind from his new bestie, McGee girded up his loins to try his first shower in prison. The unit's shower had twenty shower heads, all functional, which seemed little short of miraculous to McGee. The shower area was wide open, no private spaces or corners, for obvious security purposes. He changed into skivvies and wrapped a towel around himself. He went left to the showers; and his bestie, John went right "to take care of business."

There were two cons showering when McGee arrived at the showers, and they finished, dried off promptly, and returned to their houses. That left McGee alone which seemed like a perfect opportunity to scrape off the accumulated grime and stench of his first week in stir. He took a quick 360^0 look around him, making sure to maintain his poker face tough guy look and turned on the shower. Hot water came out in a comfortable spray, and he applied liberal amounts of his prison soap, a decent brand due to the federal requirements to supply soap during the COVID pandemic. None of the prisoners could have hand sanitizer, because it was deemed to be contraband.

He was just beginning to rinse off the cleansing and soul-uplifting suds, when he felt four powerful arms wrapping around his still sudsy, oily, slippery, and dripping wet, body. McGee reacted with practiced suddenness and ferocity. He whirled about, and all four arms lost their purchase. The muscular portion of the outside of his right fist connected with the side of one man's upper neck, and the man dropped to the inch deep water on the shower floor unconscious. McGee's torque energy continued until his hand smashed the second man's nose which produced a scream of pain and a gout of blood which put him out of the contest temporarily.

A third man did a spear block into McGee's abdomen and tackled him to the floor. A fourth brute leaped full force on McGee's chest and upper belly, pinning him. It was becoming difficult to breathe, but his will to fight was not yet quelled. The man with the broken nose was determined to vent his murderous rage, and he fell on McGee pounding his fists into the struggling man's face. McGee could not move the weights on his chest, abdomen, and thighs; and his vision became dim; and his ability to think or to call upon his muscle memory to mount a defense.

"Don't kill him," the bearded one said.

They were all festooned with white supremacy tattoos and were all big, powerful men. The bearded one grabbed a mop handle.

"We finish what we came for and why we get the big bucks. He has to live, and he has to be able think and speak. The boss made that crystal clear."

The mention of boss and money in the same sentence made a difference. What did they care; none of them had ever met the guy, let alone knew him. They methodically did what they came to do. They raped him repeatedly with the mop handle until there was sufficient bleeding to convince them that it was time to disappear. They dragged their fellow gang member back to the portion of the cell block owned by the Peckerwoods, taking care to be sure there was blood enough in the shower to make the news and to teach the newbie something about who ruled the roost.

McGee came around in the infirmary two days later with no recollection of what had happened after he walked into the shower area. He hurt all over, places he had never hurt before. He was swathed in bandages; his face was swollen and blackened. He had a painful dressing over his nose.

He moaned in pain when he became aware enough to recognize the existence of his perineum.

"Gotta lotta pain down there in Australia?" the infirmary trustee asked, not in the expected malign voice used by everyone everywhere else in the joint. "Wanna have some good stuff? It'll help."

"What happened to me?" McGee managed.

"You don't wanna know, trust me," the trustee said gently.

"Oh, yes, I do. I want to know every little detail, nothing left out."

"Look, Guy, that's above my pay grade. I only make 65 cents an hour. I'll get the doc. Want some morphine or a shot a Demerol?"

McGee was writhing in pain; he managed to croak out, "Morphine… please."

CHAPTER NINE

SAGE ADVICE

The trustee was left holding the bag. McGee got no pain medication because the doctor never came, because there was a severe shortage in every aspect of inmate medical care because COs were required for escort security, and hundreds of them failed to show up every day. There were deaths related to what amounted to a collapse in basic jail operation.

"Look, Bro, I'm sorry; I really am. So far as I can tell, ain't no doctors. Take a look around, ain't no COs either. I don't have no access to hard narcotics or even the worthless acetaminophen. I got calls out all over the place. It's rotten what you're goin' through, but it ain't my fault. Oh, I forgot. You got a visitor."

"Me? I thought the whole world had forgotten who or where I am. Is it okay if you bring my visitor to me; I'm in no shape to go anyplace else."

The trustee brought in a slender, greying, late-middle-aged man in a dark three-piece pinstripe suit and half glasses. He had a furrowed face full of worry-lines and an aquiline nose.

"I am Yitzchak Zalman Teidlemam. You may remember seeing me on zoom during your arraignment."

"I do. I'm glad you found me."

"It wasn't easy. I could not get any information using your name. Luckily for us both, I was in possession of your DAT sheet which had your prison number Number NYPD 10451-05222022 FEL-M,1."

"That's what I am reduced to, I guess."

"I wanted to talk law and strategy, but the good trustee told me about your more immediate situation. I will use my time today to find you a doctor. This place is a disgrace."

"I have terrible pain, Counselor. And, I am not much of a guy to complain. Also, I can't... uh... use number two."

"I understand that you have a serious reason not to be able to defecate. I will have a proctological surgeon in here to see you today, or my name is not Yitzack.

The attorney quickly and briefly brought McGee up to date on the fingerprint evidence against him and the investigations under way. He patted McGee on the arm and gave him a sad, consoling smile. He left and walked briskly out of the infirmary, fully bent on his mission to find a decent doctor.

It was a day for visitors. The warden himself came to visit an hour later.

"Tell me what happened to you, Number NYPD 10451-05222022 FEL-M,1. I understand you were assaulted."

Aware that this encounter was not going to be about sympathy or help, McGee gave the warden the facts as he knew them.

"Recognize any of them?"

"No."

"What can you tell me about them? White, Black, or Hispanic? Approximate ages? Identifying tattoos? I see that you haven't been here long enough to get inked. Are you gang affiliated?"

McGee concentrated on the questions, and tried to give an orderly set of answers, "I was assaulted in my anus in the showers by men using a mop handle and was also beaten nearly to death. As for the rest of your questions: No, Nothing, White, Thirties, all tattooed—they only ones I recognized were AB—and No."

He went too fast for the warden, but his traveling secretary was taking notes as always. He read back both the questions and the answers.

The warden listened then said, "That's not enough, and you know it. I think you are keeping things from me for fear of the gang members who did this to you. That's foolish. We can put you in segregation for the rest of your stay here, if you are willing to give me what I need to know."

"I have told you the truth, Warden. I do not know who did this. If I did, I might be able to avoid them in the future. Sorry, Sir."

The warden gave McGee a long dubious gaze before he and his secretary exited the infirmary.

The trustee waited until the warden was gone then said, "No likelihood of help there. Look, you didn't ask me for no advice, but I'll give you some for free. You done good by not fingering anybody. You would be a dead man by the end of the day if you hadda done. There was a message in what happened to you. Almost certainly came from the outside; somebody don't like you or don't like what you know. So, keep your lips zipped. Let me tell you something that won't seem obvious to you right now. Not everybody in stir is ganged-up. You're a newbie, and you've been tested. The rest of the gangs'll leave you alone because you obeyed the omerta. All's you have to do is have eyes in the back of your head for the four guys that done you."

"I really don't know who attacked me. How can I protect myself?"

"Two ways… well, maybe three. First, if you're a billionaire, you can pay a tax to onna the gangs for protection. The cost will go up every month, but the deals are usually honored. Second, you can go into segregation with the 'others'—guys who kiss other guys, and the loonies. And, third, you can check out the grapevine for who done this, and you can pay for a hit. Not a great idea because the hitters sometimes forget who pays them, or they leak to the gangs and the guys who done it, and you're toast."

McGee pondered for a minute.

"Look, I don't even know your name. Mine's McGee, but you already know that. Can you get the names and IDs of the guys who attacked me? You seem to be in the know about pretty much everything around here."

"I can, but I strongly advise against it. You try and off onna those mobsters, and they whole bunch'll come after you. You will have to sleep with one eye open for the rest of your life."

"That's okay. I'll take the risk."

"It'll cost you plenty."

"How about if I give you my entire cigarette ration for the rest of the time I'm in here? It looks like I'll be here until I am old and grey."

"All right, it's your funeral. I'll nose around. I should have everything you need to know before they release you back into Gen-Pop."

"Deal."

The doctor—a renowned proctological surgeon—was escorted into the infirmary at four in the afternoon, accompanied by Mr. Teitlebaum.

"This is Doctor Zedekiah Moses Heidlman, the best surgeon at the best hospital–Long Island Jewish Medical Center. With my help on the legal end, he's going take good care of you. Do you agree to be transferred today?"

"I'll say. Dr. Heidlman, could you possibly order me some morphine. The pain is doing me in," McGee asked.

"I will make that happen. A couple of questions first: has anyone examined you?"

"No."

"Do you still have blood coming out of your anus?"

"Yes."

"Cramping?"

"Yes."

"Have you been able to move your bowels or passed gas since the attack?"

"No."

"Let me take a quick look at your belly."

Dr. Heidlman was gentle as he palpated McGee's belly. Inadvertently McGee screamed in agony when the doctor pushed on the right lower quadrant of his abdomen.

"Sorry, Doc."

"No need to be. What that was is called a "chandelier sign". I touch you, and you jump off the bed and swing from the chandelier. With that, constant, severe abdominal pain, a high fever [104°], anal bleeding, and a generally bloated belly, we have an acute belly—peritonitis and a bowel obstruction–going here. This is an acute emergency. We will have you out of here within the hour if I have to call out the national guard."

"Trustee, call the warden and get him over here, *tout suite*! Tell him we have an acute medical emergency and that Mr. McGee needs immediate surgery at Long Island Jewish Medical Center. We will need an ambulance, lights and sirens. Tell me if you meet any road blocks."

"Yes, Sir," he said and ran to the phone.

He returned in less than five minutes, "Can't be done. This man is too dangerous to transport."

Dr. Heidlman removed his iphone from his left inside suit pocket and tapped in a number.

"Mayor's office."

"This is Zedekiah Heidlman, I am at Rikers; and I have an emergency case here. The warden is impeding progress on a bogus claim. I personally vouch for the patient... name of McGee. I need the warden to get a call from the Gracie Mansion ASAP."

Ten seconds later, Mayor Oglemann came on the line.

"This you, Zed?"

"It is. Look, I don't have time to chat. I just need to have you cut through the red tape and nonsense and help me get this poor guy out of here. I'll give you all the details during the poker game on Saturday night."

"Good enough, Zed. Consider it done."

Five minutes later, a call came to the infirmary from the warden's office authorizing the immediate transfer. Ten minutes later, the ambulance crew swept into the room and lifted McGee to their gurney, shackled him by both wrists and ankles and around his abdomen to the security rails, and hurried him out to the waiting ambulance.

The trustee scratched his head, "ain't what ya know, it's who ya know."

CHAPTER TEN

TAKING CARE OF BUSINESS

A month later, McGee was back in the jail infirmary convalescing from his emergency surgery. The broom handle had perforated his rectum in two places spilling feces into his pelvis. Dr. Heidlman and his OR crew had opened a midline incision from two inches above the navel to the pubis, found the perforations and infected bowel and a pelvis [notably the Space of Retzius], filled with green pus and frank feces.

The perforated bowel could not be safely repaired; so, they excised the tattered and infected segment and did an end-to-end anastomosis, which was a risk for ongoing infection; but the tears would have made a colostomy too low for optimum function. They irrigated the pelvis with gallons of sterile normal saline and Imipenem Solution to attack the ongoing intraabdominal infection and to decrease surgical site infections. They left an infusion/removal set of drains in place and irrigated the deep site for nearly a month. McGee also had a PICC line [Peripherally Inserted Central Catheter] for infusion of his toxic antibiotics—especially Azithromycin and Vancomycin.

His post-operative course was complicated by a urinary tract infection, two infections each of MERSA [Methicillin Resistant Staphylococcus Aureus] and C. diff [Clostridioides difficile or C. difficile] infection of the bowel related to eradication of the normal bowel flora and yeast infections of his Perineum, bladder, and anorectal bowel, by the treating antibiotics. It was a rocky and fraught period, but not one that came as a surprise to his surgeons or hospitalists. He was a healthy middle-aged man in good health to begin with, and he weathered all the bacterial world could throw at him.

McGee was a determined rehab patient, and he struggled against pain and exhaustion with his PT to regain his pre-operative strength and vitality. He had an incentive, and physical power was going to be an imperative. The doctors, nurses, and infirmary trustees, could only keep him for two full months before the warden intervened and ordered him back to Gen-Pop. His house—No. 934.

He kept to himself mostly. He made a point to find and locate the four gangsters who had injured him without them knowing he was shadowing them. His expensive trustee friend had combed the jail grapevine and cautiously included and eliminated them down to four certain choices. McGee stealthily hid his shiv—also a gift from the trustee—very carefully outside his cell and without the knowledge of his cellie or any other inmates.

After going over the events leading up to his object rape, he pondered every second and minute, every memory, every suspicion.

The cellie was too curious about him, and he asked too many questions. McGee asked for a swap of cellmates which took a couple of weeks but ended up with him receiving an inmate who had too easily yielded to homosexual attacks, and the warden ordered that he bunk with McGee, knowing that the slathering inmates would leave him alone as long as he was McGee's roomie. After all, the new guy— Cary Snelling—had never been seen to kiss another guy— the clear sign of being a girly man in the Gen-Pop.

He followed his four attackers to learn their routine. They were Alfred "Connie" deConstanzo, Danny "Big Ears" Clyde, Jack "Thug" Jasperson, and Derek "Odessa mafia," Bondarenko. Prison is boring, and most cons adopt habit patterns for a number of reasons: to locate or sell contraband, to hook up with sexual partners on the DL, to get maximum exercise during yard time, or to avoid exertion any time. It took three months of monotonous patience to be able to discern clear and reliable movement patterns of the four perps.

It was "Odessa mafia"'s turn first. Bondarenko was a nut for sunbathing. Whenever he could, he stretched out on the lawn near where his gang-members held sway. Comfortable in the knowledge that he was in the company and protection of friends who had vicious reputations, he often slept away the full hour with as much skin exposed as possible.

McGee ventured as near as he could. On that day and that particular time, a fight conveniently broke out twenty yards from the sunbather, and the ABs went to watch the show. McGee fetched his shiv from its hidey hole between two loose bricks near the door to the RMSC [Rose M. Singer Center] cell block. He nonchalantly meandered by Bondarenko close enough to determine that the sunburned con was fast asleep—maybe on drugs.

He faced away from the fight and its spectators, bent over, and made a quick swipe of the blade through the man's trachea and right carotid artery and large jugular veins. Bondarenko was unable to make a sound more than a brief gurgling, and he bled to death while McGee wiped off the shiv on the Odessa Mafia's bare chest and his own fingerprints and tucked his shif back in its hidey-hole.

No one saw McGee kill Bondarenko; or if they did, they complied with the prison yard omerta. The next lucky winner was Jack "Thug" Jasperson, a weight-lifting enthusiast, who concentrated overly on his biceps which were huge, disproportional, and developed at the expense of his pecs, triceps, abs, and back. He was in a zone of Zen when he lifted, grunted, and sweated, with pleasure. His eyes were closed, and he had a beatific smile on his ugly face as he struggled with a heavier weight. He was standing doing curls when McGee slipped up behind and rammed the shiv deep into his left vertebro-chondral junction, through his thoracic aorta, and into his kidney, with a twisting motion [stab, then twist]. The pain was too severe to allow him to cry out, and he died before his brain could register what had happened to him. McGee lowered him to the grass. He had mastered the prison technique of post murder invisibility.

The revenge aspect of his premeditated killings would not have been complete without taking out "Big Ears" Clyde in the shower. The man was a shower addict. He thought of showers as his only physical pleasure during his long lonely day-and-night bit. He was showering at one end of the rack of 20 showers, and six other young guys were playing "pop-the-butt" with wet towels at the other end, oblivious to Big Ears and then to McGee when he slipped in and stood directly in front of the huge thug whose face and head were covered with soap.

McGee rammed the eight-inch-long blade upwards through the space below his sternum and ripped it back and forth to slash Big Ears' diaphragm, stomach, esophagus, and the tip of his heart. He held the big man up as he struggled to breathe, to shout, to swear, or to will the massive internal bleeding to stop. He was unsuccessful, and he died quietly. McGee washed off any blood that had gotten to his orange jump suit and returned to his cell complaining to the CO of feeling sick, "must have spent too much time in the sun too soon after surgery".

McGee cornered Alfred "Connie" deConstanzo, and Jack "Thug" Jasperson as they were finishing shooting up doses of particularly pure heroin in the darkest part of the island behind OBCC [Otis Bantum Correctional

Center]. They had made the error of being habitual about time and place. It was only going to be a matter of time before the guards discovered them and sent the two lifers to the hole.

But, McGee got to them first. The two men were deep into "la-la" land when McGee moved silently through the inky blackness carrying a purloined 10 inch-bladed fireman's pickax and stepped up beside them. Each man received a single fatal head blow with the pick end that penetrated all the way to the brain stem.

Early on, it was thought that the two lifers had escaped somehow, and a manhunt outside the jail was carried out for three days until an unfortunate elderly mother of an inmate took a little walk to get some air and found them. It was the ugliest thing she had ever seen, and it made her see her violent son in an entirely new light.

McGee washed the axe and replaced it in its rack. It was never identified as the murder weapon. He tossed his shiv into a trash truck as it was leaving via the lane outside the south fence. It was never discovered. He avoided the areas where his tormenters and victims had been housed or spent their yard time, and they avoided him with grudging respect. No one ever said a thing; everyone knew who had killed the vicious bullying thugs and were glad it had happened. McGee never had another negative encounter with an inmate or guard during his months of stay on the island. He was something of a prison hero who had earned respect.

He also earned a coveted prison job—cleaning the showers, something for which the inmate participants felt genuine pride. As strange as it may seem, inmates are germophobes. It is an unspoken dictum that cleanliness is next to godliness, and a daily shower is a must. In fact, if a con takes a shower only once every three days, the other inmates will carry them into the shower with their clothes on and make them shower—make them smell better. McGee soon became the boss of the shower cleaning crew.

He saw to it that the crew always got the right chemicals, proper abrasive cleaning cloths that did not scratch the shower heads, the spigots, or handles of the sink. He learned and organized the use of ketchup to make all the metal shin without damage to metal fixtures. Accordingly, during chow time, the cleaning crew pocketed the packaged ketchup and set it aside once back in the dorm. It was the vinegar in the tomato product that did the job, but vinegar by itself was contraband. The crew followed McGee's orders with zeal and diligence to keep the tiles and grout shining. Approving COs supplied the Bon Ami or Comet cleanser from the laundry room in handy spray bottles. The chemicals came from the laundry room, and they came in spray bottles. The crew earned some perks—for which they credited McGee—for the superior shine to their metal.

The worst of the worst thugs enjoyed their nice hot clean showers, and—crediting McGee—they spread the word that he was one inmate that was no problem for anyone and was to be left alone to keep his work going. As a result, an increased level of peace and security began to prevail on McGee's unit. Everyone got along and the crew all agreed with each other. That example of how to live life as a long timer made an impression and a difference.

CHAPTER ELEVEN

THE FIRST TRIAL

McGee came to the attention of the general public before his attorneys wanted him to. *The New York Times* wrote an explosive series of articles on the brutish conditions on Rikers Island, particularly with regards to deficiencies of inmate medical care. McGee was the key individual to highlight the article. The author of the NYT piece informed the public about McGee's post beating surgical emergency and that it had required direct intervention by the mayor to get that accomplished. The paper's reporters and its lawyers gave serious credence to an affidavit from the city that showed that there were more than 1,000 instances in December of that year alone in which a detainee did not make a scheduled medical appointment because a guard was not available to escort them. The city claimed that more than 5,000 times that same month, Rikers Island inmates refused to attend scheduled medical appointments.

The paper's rebuttal cast doubt on that number, and a doctor who recently left Correctional Health Services said the number was probably overblown. It was vaguely posited that the jail just might have fudged a bit because they cancelled appointments and appearances owing to Rikers' inadequacies.

Because of McGee's newly obtained prominence, the social notability of the Lythgoes—and the possible connection of Hartley Lythgoe and his Teamsters union with organized crime—along with the gruesome murder of the mystery woman–Madeleine Noémie Toussaint–in the historically significant 943 Park Avenue South building, the impending trial was gathering steam for a usual New York media circus trial. It was already being billed as the "crime of the century" despite there being only scanty knowledge of the particulars. On the first day of the trial, the streets around the Federal Court House at 500 Pearl Street Suite 8 were teeming with reporters, paparazzi, and crime aficionados, in preparation for the circus festivities. Park Row, Pearl, Worth, and Centre, Streets were an angry grid-locked parking lot.

The opening day of the United States v. McGee consisted of routine and boring meetings between the prosecution and defense attorneys with District Judge Hyman Rotweillin to decide certain evidentiary issues, stipulations, and procedures, for the trial. Most of the pre-trial attention centered on the choice of witnesses and the manner by which witnesses would be allowed to give evidence, and the identification of the many expert witnesses. The second day was taken up with voir dire—selection of the jury—which turned out be harbinger of the acrimony to come in the trial-in-chief.

The Deputy US Attorney General faced the jury with a grim face to deliver his opening:

"Ladies and Gentlemen of the jury, I am Deputy US Attorney General Franklin Caruthers, the lawyer for the people of the United States and the Southern District of New York. US Attorney General for the SDNY, Milton Weilenbach, and I will guide you through the people's case against Joseph Patrick Aloysius Michael John McGee on the charge of premeditated first-degree murder."

He was brief and presented a list of evidence against McGee and witnesses scheduled to testify.

"We are confident that you, the members of the jury, will be able to render a verdict of guilty beyond a reasonable doubt based on that evidence and do your part to keep a dangerous murderer off our streets. Thank you for your service."

Mr. Teitlebaum was about to rise from his seat to object to the part about "doing their part to keep a dangerous murderer off our streets", but he thought better of it and relaxed.

When it was his turn, Teitlebaum began with a smile and genial expression, determined to get the jury on his side and on McGee's side from the start.

"I am the attorney for the defense, name's Teitlebaum. Now, I wouldn't like to cast aspersions on my learned colleague…" he said with something of a mischievous smile, "but, he has a case supported by minimal and inadequate evidence. He has no eye witnesses, no GSR on my client's person or clothing; that's gun shot residue. He did not fire a gun. There are no fingerprints from my client anywhere connected to anything but an improvised box used as a weapon and on the handle of a machete, the murder weapon in the second case. Don't you find that a bit odd? Nowhere else. Oh, and both fingerprints were identical, pristine perfect, and perfectly placed.

Don't you find that to be more than a bit odd? The defense will present witnesses and evidence which will cast serious, even beyond, reasonable doubt on the prosecution's evidence. Ladies and Gentlemen of the jury, when I do, you will feel duty, morally, and legally, bound to declare my fine client not guilty beyond reasonable doubt. This has been a short opening, because this is a case with such limited evidence. I plan to get you home early today, and to have this be a brief trial for the same reasons… unless you want to vote now for a long drawn-out affair…"

He gave a wry smile, and the jury actually laughed out loud. The taciturn old judge allowed a very brief grin to crack the stone of his face.

It was three o'clock in the afternoon.

Judge Rotweillin admonished the jury to speak to no one about anything related to the case and to come on time the following day at ten a.m. sharp ready to hear the prosecution begin its case. The jury smiled at each other and a few even smiled a sort of obtuse thanks for the respite in Teitlebaum's direction. He modestly nodded his head in recognition.

The first witness for the prosecution was NYPD Lead task force Detective First Class Kyle Ritchens. After introducing the detective to the jury and giving a list of his accomplishments, time in service, honors, and medals including: Police Combat Cross, Medal for Valor, MPD [Meritorious Police Duty], EPD [Excellent Police Duty], Unit Citation, Purple Shield, and Distinguished Service Medal, Deputy US Attorney, Franklin Caruthers began his Q & A.

Q: Is it correct that you have been the lead detective for the two sets of murders—nine in all—including Henry Kendall Lythgoe, President of Local Union No. 295 International Brotherhood of Teamsters and his wife, Mary Margaret O'L. Lythgoe, their unborn child, and Madeleine Noémie Toussaint?

A: Yes.

Q: Would you relate the findings you and your task force made, the evidence found, and how these two crimes are related.

Richens did so fairly briefly but in gruesome detail, which was accompanied by visual aids in all their gory elements of the crime scene. The photos and 360⁰ video presentation brought gasps and hands over faces from the jury and spectators. He linked the two crime scenes by stating that indisputable fingerprint evidence against JPAMJ McGee was found in very incriminating areas of each crime scene. The timing of the murders was close to the same time period with plenty of time for McGee to have traveled between scenes and done the crime.

Q: Did the defendant confess?

A: Not to us.

Q: Did you find evidence that caused you to suspect anyone else of having done the crimes, had a motive to do so, or to have acted as accomplices?

A. No.

Q. As you are aware, Detective, motive is not legally required to establish evidence in a crime, but do you have evidence indicating that Mr. McGee had motive to kill the decedents?"

A: No.

"Nothing further."

Teitlebaum cross examined the detective.

Q: How would you describe the quality and condition of the fingerprint evidence, Detective?

A: Excellent, no question about who left the prints and the importance of where they were left.

Q: The ME's report for both scenes used the word "perfect". Would you agree with that?

A. I would.

Q: Did you see the fingerprint evidence yourself?

A: I did.

Q: What was your personal opinion, since I am sure that in your long service you have had a chance to observe many sets of prints?

A: As clear or even better than any set I have ever seen. There was absolutely no doubt about the owner of the prints, the location, or the significance.

Q: Did you find it remarkable or even odd that you found two sets of perfect and identical prints in two separate crime scenes in the same week.

A: Not, really. Sometimes even cops catch a break.

"Nothing further at this time, but I would like to reserve the right to recall Detective Ritchens," Teitlebaum said.

"Granted," the judge said, "Detective, I remind you that you will remain under oath and that you are not to discuss any element of this case outside the investigation task force or the prosecution. Do you understand?"

"I do."

"Call your next witness, Mr. Caruthers."

"The prosecution calls the Medical Examiner, Doctor Lincoln Ackinson."

Dr. Atkinson described his thirty-year career, his education, experience, and honors, in answer to his first question and a forty- minute description of the condition of the murder victims, the manner of death, and the best approximation of the times of both occurrences:

"for the killings in the lobby of the Hilton Garden Inn Times Square, 790 Eighth Avenue, we can be precise: 1214 hours, as determined by the best witness we have found and the wall clock that stopped at the instant of the explosion. For the murder in the penthouse at

443 Park Avenue South Condominiums—57th and Park Avenue, Midtown Manhattan—96th floor, the time was somewhere between 0200 and 0600 the morning before the Hilton murders. We cannot be more precise because the victim had the air conditioning going at near-freezing all night."

On cross, Teitlebaum asked a series of brief questions:

Q: Thank you, Dr. Atkinson. I will not question your fine credentials, I am impressed by them. I ask, what was your opinion regarding the finding of two sets of what have been called "perfect prints" in two different crime scenes? Was that coincidence?

A: I don't believe in coincidence, Counselor; I believe in cause and effect. I must say it is remarkable to have found such good prints, but not out of the realm for reasonable occurrence.

Q: How do you explain the marked differences between the two scenes: the one a carefully planned and executed assassination, and the other a frenzied hacking and slashing?

A: That would suggest two different murderers except for the fingerprint evidence. The first "frenzied" murder, as you call it, or an "overkill" as police and MEs usually describe it, may represent the act of a seriously upset or disturbed individual who calmed down enough to carry out the second crime. There does not seem to be evidence to indicate a murder-for-hire, or the act of a willing accomplice, again given the same fingerprint evidence.

Q. Could the first murder have been committed later in the day, closer to the time of the second?

A. Not at all likely. The cold would have skewed the time as being later than it was. It would be the opposite as your question posited.

"Thank you, Dr. Atkinson, no further questions for this witness."

"The prosecution calls CSI Lacy Hicken.

CSI Hicken was a frequent member of the federal prosecution teams to testify about crime scenes, and she appeared to be calm, assured, and thoroughly competent professional. Her hair was done in a severe pull back bun, and her clothing—a crisp grey two piece-suit, sensible shoes, a light grey silk blouse.

She gave the usual credentialling information and Teitlebaum did not question its authenticity or pertinence.

Q: Now, CSI Hicken, please describe the two crime scenes, one at a time, and explain the meaning of the findings in terms of evidence, and differences between the two.

She did.

Q: Did you see the fingerprints in situ? For the jury, that means, "in place"?

A: I did.

Q. Give us your impression, please.

A: I saw them in situ and after they had been lifted. It would have been easy to read them as they were found; they were that clear. I was party to the AFIS data as well.

There could be no possibility of error. Those prints were from the defendant, Mr. McGee.

Q: How did the prints get to the place you found them?

A: In each instance, they were placed by the defendant at the time of the murder; they were on the murder weapon in each case.

"Objection. Lacks foundation."

"Sustained, rephrase, Mr. Caruthers."

Q. In your rather vast experience CSI Hicken, what is the most likely way for fingerprints to be found on murder weapons?

A: Placed there by the perp.

"Nothing further."

Teitlebaum was again brief in cross-examination.

Q: Just two question, CSI Hicken. First, do you agree with the previous testimonies that have been given in this court that the prints were "perfect"?

A: As near perfect as I have ever seen or know about.

Q: Second, have any fingerprints ever been found to be identical between two persons, say, in identical twins?"

A: No. It is one of the foundations of fingerprint evidence that prints are different for every human being who ever lived without exception, even for identical twins.

Q: Is it not odd that the prints in question are so pristine... so "perfect" as you put it. How would one intentionally place his or her fingerprints in order to give to the police such perfect and complete fingerprints... two times in a row?

Hicken paused for a moment to think.

"Take your time, Ms. Hicken," Teitlebaum said quietly.

A: In my experience, a person would have had to be very precise and careful about the placement location, the right amount of pressure, and above all, that he or she did not make the slightest movement while placing the prints.

Q: Does that jibe with the findings in these cases, especially the Toussaint murder? How do you account for that?

A: There are millions of fingerprints left all over all the time. By chance, two of the millions could have met the criteria you described.

Q: By chance!!?? Twice!!?? In a single week!!??

He asserted the emphasis without raising his voice.

A: That is what I surmise. I can only go by the evidence... by the truth as I, as a scientist, know it.

Q: Really, it is left to chance?

"Objection. Asked and answered, your Honor."

"The jury will disregard the most recent question, and it will be stricken from the transcript."

Teitlebaum sat stoically in his seat, mum.

"Next witness, Mr. Caruthers. We have forty-five minutes. Can you finish in that much time?"

"Yes, your Honor."

He got an "okay" nod from the judge.

"The prosecution calls FBI fingerprint specialist, Special Agent Dermount G. Dorrity."

The agent was a diminutive bespectacled man in a regulation blue suit, white shirt, and tie the same color as his suit, and shiny black oxford wingtip shoes all of which was quintessentially FBI agent ware of a bygone era. It readily identified him as a lifer agent, an analyst rather than a field agent, and a geek.

Dorrity was good, nearly perfect, in his demeanor, recitation of his education, experience, and authority within the bureau.

Q: Did you have an opportunity to examine finger-print evidence in the two cases, New York, Lythgoe, and Toussaint v. McGee, the subjects of this trial?

A: I did.

Q: Please tell us your findings. Don't be offended if I ask you to explain some arcane finding you describe to make everything clear for the jury.

A: You will not have to do that, Counselor. This is not the first time I have described a fingerprint, nor the first time I have testified to nonexpert jurors. Please try not to interrupt the flow of my dialogue.

Chagrined, the deputy US Attorney held his piece while Dorrity dialogued.

True to his word, he had a script that catered to both the expert and the novice regarding fingerprinting in general, and in the two cases on trial.

A: In short, no one can reasonably doubt that the fingerprints found at the crime scenes belonged to one Joseph, Patrick, Aloysius, Michael, John McGee. They were placed by him on the murder weapons. They place him at the scene, at the time, and with the very act. I have never been more certain of fingerprint evidence in my career as I am in this instance."

"No further questions."

Teitlebaum stood up to do his cross, the only time during the questioning of the day.

"Thank you, Dr. Dorrity… that is the correct title isn't it.?

"Yes. I am not a medical practitioner, but rather a "real doctor" as scholars, researchers, and universities, characterize us. In the UK, medical practitioners are rightly called, Mister, particularly the surgeons. It has to be with the PhD process, one of original research, and a rigorous education culminating in the defense of a carefully done dissertation."

Q: Again, thank you, Dr. Dorrity, for the enlightenment. Now, to my questions. Would you be so kind as to display on the screen the fingerprints you studied and why you regard them so highly as evidence?

A: Of course.

Dr. Dorrity proceeded to talk and point at the same time using the clear fingerprints displayed for the benefit of his rapt audience, the jury. He discussed and pointed out crossovers, cores, bifurcations, ridge endings, deltas, dots, terminations, spurs, bridges, snort ridges, pores, and islands, and explained the evident crispness of the display before the jury.

He emphasized the core principles of fingerprints: the individuality of the characteristics, the unique patterns, and that they do not change over a person's life.

"There are no two people with the same prints, including in the minuteauie described just now. So, there are not mistakes in that regard… ever! Dermatoglyphics is an exact science, at least in the eyes and hands of experts. Dermatoglyphics is a heritable trait that is considered as a usual phenotype in criminology. There are links and types of prints found with certain blood groups.

We went so far as to check Mr. McGee's prints against his blood type—A+. The fingerprint pattern in Rh blood types of blood group "A" is statistically significant while in others it is insignificant. In middle and little fingers, loops were higher whereas in ring finger whorls were higher in all *other* blood groups. Mr. McGee's prints were perfect exemplars of his blood type and exactly what we would expect from the man."

Teitlebaum noted that the members of the jury were fighting to keep their eyes open. He sympathized with them and was pleased that the tidy little man and the prosecutor had fallen into the trap of boring the jury and losing their interest.

"Thank you for your enlightening testimony, Dr. Dorrity. I have no further questions for this witness."

Teitlebaum stood up and gave the jury a wry, complicit, smile.

"Sorry, Ladies and Gentlemen of the jury. I am sure your brains are as fried as mine; so, I promise to be brief."

Several jury members gave him a thankful smile. One man, an authoritarian looking, well-dressed fellow, gave him an icy glare. Teitlebaum was not sure what to make of that.

Q: No such thing as identical fingerprints in different people, Sir?

A: No. I think I have made that perfectly clear.

Q: How likely do you think it would be that the two sets of fingerprints would have been placed so carefully and precisely during two separate murders, as described by the experienced crime scene investigator, Ms. Hicken?

A: She is a technologist; I am a PhD and a senior FBI agent. Consider the source. However, I do admit that the woman made valid observations about the fingerprints and their presence in conjunction with the crime scene evidence.

"Thank you, Dr. Dorrity. You have been most helpful. No further questions."

"Court is adjourned until tomorrow morning at ten, when the prosecution will continue its case… hopefully not for very long."

And he banged his gavel bringing on grateful relieved smiles and sighs from the weary jury.

CHAPTER TWELVE

THE INVESTIGATORS INVESTIGATE, AND THE PROSECUTION RESTS

The partners hired a retired private investigator to attend every minute McGee's trial was in session and to take meticulous notes. They had more pressing work to do. At the very onset of the involvement of McGee, they became certain that there was nothing random or coincidental about the killings, and there was something that purposefully linked McGee to the crimes. In their quick conferences together, they became more and more convinced—as a working thesis—that this was a gang caper, at least gang related. Their evidence for that was scanty, but they had nothing more to go on. The police had essentially closed their investigation and accepted McGee's guilt despite the limited but damning evidence. Ivory and Caitlin were convinced that McGee was being used as a patsy.

~119~

Ivory was able to convince his onetime gang—the Black Knights—to see the arrest and trial of McGee as something that involved them at least peripherally. Besides, the BK had used McGee and Associates to get to the bottom of a few of their more knotty problems and to prevent wars in Harlem. Damien Markee, who was once the number one in the BK [Black Knights]–and now is probably one of the head honchos of the Luccheses–had a past with McGee and seemed to be genuinely bent out of shape at the injustice. He told Ivory that the Luccheses were at his service.

"Damien, I have an idea," Ivory said. "We need some leverage against the Genoveses who are about the only people who would seem to have something to gain by off-ing Lythgoe and maybe even the woman, Toussaint, and implicating McGee as well. He helped your Luccheses to gain the upper hand in Manhattan for the legit garment business. What you did about the not-so-legit was none of our business. Whatever, the Genoveses did not like you or us over the affair. You have some inside connection in the NYPD that could give us the dope on some relatively minor Genovese who gets sideways with the cops and might be looking for a way out as a snitch or giving evidence against one of the higher-ups. I think we could find a way to turn the cops' attention towards the Lythgoe and Toussaint murders. We could make it worth your while."

"I'll see what I can come up with."

The trial resumed at ten on the dot the next day with the first witness, Gladys Owens Perkins, the duped tourist from Kansas City, Kansas. Actually, Deputy Attorney General Franklin Caruthers had little hope that she would enhance his case, but he was duty-bound to question her since she was the only witness who could cast any light on events immediately prior to the murders.

Q: Mrs. Owens, the people of New York wish to thank you for making the trip back here to New York.

A: It is my civic duty, Sir.

Q: In your own words, please tell us what happened at the Hilton Hotel that eventful day.

A: Well… the hubby and me wanted to see the Big City; so's, he went to the Mets game; he's a big fan. I wanted to walk around the busy streets, pretend to be shopping with all the city swells, and to take in the skyscrapers. I was standing, chewing on a New York beg…al looking in the big window into the lobby of the Hilton Garden Inn Hotel Times Square… at 790 Eighth Avenue. A nice looking… kinda Mexican looking, you know, sort of man dressed in a nice suit come acrost to me and saw I was taking some photos.

'Nice camera, you got,' he says. He was nice. We talked for about a minute about cameras, and he showed me his, a weird sort of box thing. He says I look like a nice sort of lady and asks me if I would mind taking a picture of a man and his wife who would be in the lobby. He was a newspaper photographer, he says, and they wouldn't let him take any photos in the hotel on account of he was from the press. He was going to lose his job if he couldn't get a picture; it was the man's birthday, and it was going to be in the Society Section. I said, 'sure'; and he showed me how to work the camera thing. It was disguised; so, no one would realize it was a camera. Alls I had to do was to squeeze a little gizmo. I didn't even have to look through a lens or nothing. Just point at his chest and squeeze. Nothing hard about that.

Q: What did you do next, Mrs. Owens?

A: I walked into the lobby like I owned the place. Nobody paid me no mind. I done just like the nice man told me. I stood in the middle of the lobby and waited for the important man and his pretty wife to come into view. They was all dolled-up, and she was carrying a birthday gift.

Q: What happened next?

A: I done like the man said. Pointed the camera/box at the man's chest and mashed the gizmo. The strangest thing happened, you know. The camera thing shot a bullet out and hit the big man square in the chest, and he dropped just like you would expect. I was flabbergasted.

Q: Was that all?"

A: Not be a long shot. The pretty lady got a terrible white look on her face and dropped her present to the floor. Then, the thing blowed up… a real big explosion. Blowed up most of the whole lobby, and I figgered the ruuf, knocked me on my kiester, pardon my French. My ears was ringing like crazy for more'n a hour. I was on the floor, next thing I knew. There was screaming and smoke and pieces of the walls and furniture flying around. I must've plumb blacked out because the next thing I knew a police lady was asking me if I was okay.

Q: Did you know the man or woman who died?

A: Nope.

Q: The man who gave you the box?

A: Him neither. Never seen him before.

Q: Did he tell you anything about wanting Mr. and Mrs. Lythgoe dead?

A: Not a word.

"Thank you. No further questions.

Teitlebaum gave Mrs. Owens a friendly down-home smile and asked a few questions of his own.

"Nice of you to give up your time for us New Yorkers. Must have been quite a shock, your first trip to the Big Apple.

She spoke with a unique Midwestern accent, "You can say that again. I'll never forget dis if I live to be a hundred."

Q: Did the police take you to the station and ask you questions?

A: You be…tcha—with the word in a diphthong—sounds made up of two vowels—in words with only one vowel present–More'n a hour's worth.

Q: Did they take you to see what they call a "line-up"?

A: Sure did. You oughta know; you was there, I remember.

Q: Did you identify anyone as the man you talked to?

A: Nope.

Q: Did you identify the man who is on trial here, Mrs. Owens?

A: Nope. Which one is he?

Q: He is sitting in the defense area.

A: The skinny guy with the bad suit?

Q: No, the other man.

A: Never seen neither of dem… never.

"Thank you, Mrs. Owens, you have been very helpful. No further questions."

McGee had been brought from the Tombs, put in a suit, and stood in the lineup. Now, he was sitting by Teitlebaum's investigator, and both of them were wearing their best expressionless poker faces. McGee's wrists were in handcuffs; so, he kept his hands on his lap under the defense table.

"Call your next witness, Mr. Caruthers."

"The prosecution calls Jacob Washington Hartwell.

Hartwell–McGee's one time cellmate–swore on the Bible to tell the truth, the whole truth, and nothing but the truth.

Q: Mr. Hartwell, what is your occupation?

A: Corporate accountant.

Q: What is your present residence?"

A: Rikers Island jail.

Q: Have you been convicted of a crime?

A: Yes. Fraud.

Q: Have you ever committed or been convicted of perjury?

A: No.

Q: Are you acquainted with the defendant, Mr. McGee?

A: Yes, we were cellmates for several months in Rikers.

Q: Did you ever have occasion to talk to Mr. McGee about why he was in jail?

A: Often. We became friends and confidantes. We talked freely. I almost got a little nervous because my cellmate was telling me things I probably shouldn't hear.

Q: What sorts of things?

A: Let me cut to the chase. The man bragged. He was becoming a cool dude in the jail, and it bettered his position to be known as a big-time murderer. He told me in detail how he arranged for some simple woman to shoot the Lythgoes using a contrived box gun, and how he used his underworld contacts to make a bomb. He was pretty jittery about his first murder, a woman named Toussaint. She had two-timed him, and he wanted to bump her off and put the blame on the mob—the enemies of his friends. Another mobster–one of the Genoveses—considered the woman in the penthouse to be his moll. McGee thought that guy would get the blame. When he got to her apartment, she argued, called him names, and disrespected him. He had brought along a machete to scare her with, but she made him mad. He has a hidden temper, he told me; and he lost it. He went nuts and hacked her to bits. Told me it was one of the "most exhilarating things he ever did", gave him a "real high". And that's a direct quote. As soon as I could, I put in for a transfer and got away from the loonie.

The former cellie came across as an intelligent, well-educated, tall, fit, Black, man who was very well dressed, had a fresh neat haircut, and shined oxfords. He wore expensive prescription glasses with stylish frames., The jury hung on his every word.

"Is the defense ready for cross?

"I am. I certainly am."

"Proceed, Mr. Teitlebaum."

Just a few questions for this witness from the prison."

Q: How much are you being paid to come to this courtroom to lie, Mr. Hartwell?

A: I am not being paid anything.

Q: Come now, Mr. Hartwell, do you think I was born yesterday or that the jury is a bunch of morons? You had to have gotten something—better quarters, other perks, transfer to a minimum security facility, money for your family, or maybe a reduction in your sentence. C'mon, out with it.

"Objection, badgering the witness."

"Sustained. Mr. Teitlebaum, back off to your defense table, confine your questions to those acceptable to my court's decorum.

Another such reprimand will result in you being charged with contempt."

Teitlebaum gave a sheepish little nod.

Q: Sir, did you understand my question, or would you like to have the court recorded read it back to you?

A: I got it. No money, but my sentence is being reduced by four months; so, I will be out of jail in two weeks.

Q: How nice for you. Mr. McGee never said anything remotely like you just testified to did he? You were paid well to tell the story the prosecution wants the jury to hear. Isn't that the whole truth, and nothing but the truth?

A: Yes… I mean, no. You mixed me up. I told the truth, and I stand by that.

Teitlebaum shook his head in disgust, a gesture the jury could not have missed, "No more questions for this man who has been so highly rewarded."

"With that we will adjourn for the day," Judge Rotweillin said.

"If it please the court, the prosecution rests."

CHAPTER THIRTEEN

THE DEFENSE GETS ITS TURN

Ten o'clock sharp. Everyone in their places. District Judge Hyman Rotweillin moved into the court room, and the bailiff intoned the familiar, "All rise." It is now the turn of the defense to make its case. McGee's freedom or maybe even his life depends on what is said and done over the next day or two.

"Is the defense ready?"

"Yes, your honor."

"Prosecution?"

"We are."

"Let us begin. Mr. Teitlebaum, call your first witness."

"The defense calls David Belle Jordan."

After he was sworn in, Teidlebaum asked Jordan if he had volunteered to be a witness, and the Chief of D's answered with an emphatic "No", he had been subpoenaed. He was next asked to give his rank, police training and experience, and current position. That done, Teidle-baum went directly to the meat of the case.

Q: Were you the AO—arresting officer–in this case, Chief Jordan?"

A: Yes.

Q: Did you deliver Mr. McGee to Central Booking?"

A: Yes.

Q: Did he resist arrest?"

A: No.

Q: Did Mr. McGee confess or give any incriminating evidence about himself or the crimes?

A: No.

Q: Did he indicate that he knew the Lythgoes?

A: No

Q: Nothing?

A: We scarcely spoke.

Q: Anything about Ms. Toussaint?

A: No. I didn't even know about her.

Q: Did you witness Mr. McGee killing the Lythgoes?

A: No.

Q: Did you personally see him in the vicinity of either crime scene?

A: No.

Q: Did you question Mr. McGee about the crimes?

A: No.

Q: Then, how is it you got involved as the arresting officer, Chief Jordan? Didn't seem more than a bit thin, I mean, wasn't your police officer curiosity aroused? Isn't your involvement more than just a little unusual?

"Objection, compound question and lacking foundation," Caruthers said in a conversational voice.

"Sustained. Try again, Mr. Teitleman."

"Sorry your honor, got ahead of myself."

The questions were separated into three parts and asked and answered separately. Some of the jurors nodded as if to indicate that the repetition was intentional and for their benefit.

A: I was ordered by the commissioner of the NYPD to arrest him.

Q: And you are a good soldier and just do as you are told.

A: I am a subordinate; and yes, I obey orders.

Q: Were you even aware of any evidence against Mr. McGee?

Jordan paused to think.

A: Actually, no I wasn't at that point. I learned about the evidence later in the day.

"No further questions."

"The witness is excused, thank you for testifying Chief Jordan."

Jordan gave a slight nod to the judge and strode briskly out of the courtroom.

"Call your next witness, Mr. Teitlebaum."

"The defense calls Richard Baring Goldmann."

The attorneys at the prosecution table took a hurried scan of the witness list and gave each other quizzical looks.

Q: Dr. Goldmann please identify yourself for his honor and the jury. Give us the particulars about your education, research, and any pertinent personal and professional information related to this case.

A: I am Richard Baring Goldmann, MA, PhD, JD. I received my BA and MA degrees from the Tel Aviv University, and Hebrew University of Jerusalem, respectively. My PhD was awarded from Harvard University in criminology. My dissertation and post graduate interests have centered on criminalistics, particularly concerned with dermatoglyphics. I obtained my law degree from Stanford University in California. I am currently a professor of law specializing in criminalistics in the University of Chicago.

Q: Do you practice law?

A: I do. My practice is largely consultative, and I serve either prosecution or defense as needed. I am often called upon to give expert testimony in bench trials.

Q: Where are you a member of the bar?

A: New York, California, Illinois, and Virginia in the United States; and—consequent to my experience abroad—I am a member of the Israeli bar. I am certified as a solicitor and barrister in England, Wales, and Australia, as a result of holding a degree in the appropriate subjects, having completed the two-stage assessments, SQE1 and SQE2 and having completed the requisite two years of qualifying work experience–the QWE.

Q: Have you had the opportunity to evaluate the fingerprint evidence in this case?

A: I have.

Q: What is your opinion regard that evidence?

A: By all known standards—scientific and legal—the fingerprints belong to a person known as JPAMJ McGee, the defendant in this case. However, there are a couple of caveats.

Q: And they are?

A: First, and most arguable. is the common understanding that no two persons have or even can have identical fingerprints, and the second is a real concern of mine that these fingerprints are simply too good, better than almost any I have ever seen in a legal case.

Q: Let's deal with your first concern—whether or not people can have identical prints to each other.

A: Yes. That is a fascinating subject. Ordinarily, when making that statement, the recognized "expert" knowingly or unknowingly is referring to the unique selection of fingerprints for each human being, including differing fingerprints on different fingers. Since its invention in the 19th century, modern fingerprint identification has relied upon the assumption that by examining a person's fingerprints one can identify that individual with certainty and to the exclusion of all others. This assumption has–in turn–rested on another assumption: that no two people have fingerprints that are exactly identical in terms of the form and configuration of their patterning. It was on the basis of this notion of the individual uniqueness of fingerprints that police, forensic experts, and prison officials, have been so confident that they could identify individuals using this technique.

It is important to be clear about what "uniqueness" means in this context, however. When people make the claim that fingerprints are unique to the individual, they do not mean that there are no two people with the same number or configuration of arches, loops, and whorls on their fingers, because, in fact, there are. The uniqueness is in the minutiae.

Fingerprint minutiae or "Galton details" are defined as anatomy of ridges along a ridge path, including bifurcations-points at which one friction ridge divides into two friction ridges; dots-isolated friction ridge units that have lengths similar to their widths; and ridge endings-the abrupt end of ridges. When asked by courts for proof of the "reliability" of forensic fingerprint evidence, fingerprint examiners answered that all fingerprint patterns are unique. Courts failed to grasp the gap in logic between the two statements and uniqueness became enshrined as the foundation of the accuracy of forensic fingerprint identification. That is recognized as of this today.

Fingerprint matching, the long uncontested mark of who did or didn't do it, it turns out, has never been scientifically tested. The belief that no two humans have the same fingerprints, we learn, is not necessarily true. It's merely sounded good all the years, and we've felt pretty good about following the wisdom that this belief held. The PCAST [Presidential Council of Advisors on Science and Technology] in 2016 concluded fingerprint theory was "foundationally valid," but fingerprint analysis should never be presented in court without **evidence of its error rates** and of the proficiency or reliability of not just the method, but the particular examiner using the method. Bear that in mind in this case and all others involving fingerprint evidence.

Now, I have no bone to pick with the experts, the methodology, or the examination of these prints. My very real question is are the prints left at the scene not too good? It is too much of a coincidence in such different crime scenes and where the prints were found that the prints–which are undoubtedly those of the defendant, Mr. McGee–they are so perfect and so identical, as to consider strongly the option that they were planted.

Q: Is it your testimony in this courtroom today that the important fingerprints discovered in the crime scenes—both crime scenes—were somehow copied by persons unknown and transferred to the crime scene?

A: That is my testimony. Is it far-fetched? No more so than having me believe that two literally identical and perfectly preserved fingerprints appeared in the scenes having been carefully placed and preserved by a single person however carefully to achieve that goal not in his best interests and lead me to be most dubious about how those perfect prints got there. If I may ask a question?

"We can run by his honor to see if it is all right? Side bar, your honor?" asked Teidlebaum.

"Approach."

Teitlebaum, Caruthers, and Dr. Goldmann, stood before the judge.

"Speak softly and state your question."

"Was DNA found, and if so, did it incriminate or exonerate anyone? When I have the answer, I might make a short final note about DNA forensics."

"You may ask it."

Dr. Goldmann asked his question, and both attorneys contributed that none was identified or used. "Over time, fingerprint data is not as rock solid as its supporters would suggest. I suggest that a search for DNA is in order and should be sought forthwith."

CHAPTER FOURTEEN

SUPPING WITH THE DEVIL

Mr. Teitlebaum called his first witness for the day as soon as the preliminaries were over. He was aware of the growing weariness of the jury and was anxious to reassure them that the end was nearing. Hopefully, that would perk them up to pay attention. He was about to make the most important point in his case.

"The defense calls Agatha Horton Perkins."

With the exception of Yitzchak Teitlebaum, not another person in the courtroom had ever heard of the woman who must be the world's living greatest expert at something pertinent to the defense.

A portly middle-aged Black woman dressed in a colorful African print dress, a quintessential African-American hair style [Afro Hair–a hairstyle made up of a mass of very tight curls surrounding the head, longer in the front than it is in the back, resembling a capital "A" preserved for the occasion in an Alkaline Perm, a stronger, harsher type of permanent solution to create tight, firm curls. It has a pH level of 7.5 to 9.5]. She was wearing loose fitting pink slippers. It was apparent from her gait that she had arthritic hips and knees.

She was sworn in and stepped slowly into the witness chair.

"Good morning, Mrs. Perkins. Thank you for coming to help in the court today."

"My pleasure, Mistah Teitlebaum, thank you for axen me to be heah."

Q: Now, Mrs. Perkins; so, we can get to know you better, would you be so kind as to tell us about yourself, like where you live, your education, your occupation, and your interests?

A: Not too much to tell. I am forty-eight years old, lived in the Bronx for that whole time. I was educated in PS 197 JOHN B RUSSWURM grade school on 2230 5th Avenue, then at Harriet Tubman Charter School on third ave. for Junior High.

Q: What was the highest grade you attended, if you don't mind me asking?

A: I don' mind. Eighth grade. Harriet Tubman is a mighty fine school.

Q: I know its reputation. What is your occupation?

A: I am a proud homemaker, mother, and gramma. Twicet a week, I do some house cleaning for some swells in upper Harlem. That's about it.

Q: I understand you have a specialty hobby that you show the neighborhood schools and sometimes law enforcement. Would you tell us about that, please?

A: That's right. I do fingerprinting. I can take anybody's fingerprint and put it anywhere. When I show that to cops, makes 'em right nervous.

Q: How interesting. Your honor, may we have Mrs. Perkins do a demonstration for us?

"I have no objection. Okay with the prosecution?"

"Sure, go ahead."

Mrs. Perkins opened her large purse and retrieved an 8½' X 11' piece of white paper, a No. 2 pencil, and a roll of Scotch tape. The defense team provided a small table in the middle of room, and she set to work. She made a 2' X 2' heavy blackened area on the paper with the pencil.

Mr. Teitlebaum asked the judge if it would be permitted for the defendant to be the subject of the fingerprinting experiment, and he granted the unusual request. Mrs. Perkins smiled at McGee, and he gave her a little bow, which produced a cautious titter through the jury. Then, she expertly rolled his finger in the pencil carbon on her paper and rolled the blackened finger on another portion of her sheet. She took out a moistened dish rag from a baggie in her purse and carefully cleaned an area on the table. After that, she tore of a short piece of Scotch tape and—with steady hands—placed it on McGee's print, sticky side down. She removed the piece of tape and showed it to the jury and the prosecution. Finally, she asked a neighbor sitting in the public section to take a print. The neighbor just happened to be a crime scene analyst with an office in the Tombs admission area.

The neighbor applied a mist of cyanoacrylate [super glue, available at most hardware stores] before using powders, then dusted McGee's print with graphite-based powder to highlight the print. Next, he applied *AccuTrans*–a liquid casting compound–to lift the powdered latent prints from the desk surface. When the mold was dry, he photographed it with his iPhone camera, and displayed the digitalized image on the courtroom screen. It was a perfect match to McGee's formal print and to the prints lifted from the crime scenes. The entire process took less than five minutes. Teitlebaum offered the new print as Defense Exhibit 5.

"No further questions for this witness."

Caruthers was on the edge of laughing.

"Hello, Mrs. Perkins. I am the prosecuting attorney, that means I work for the federal government. I have very few, maybe just one question. All right with you?

"It don't make no never minds to me, Mr. Government Attorney. It's your nickel, shoot."

Q: Did you plant a fake print at our crime scenes?

A: I most certainly did not. That would be altogether wrong, a crime probably.

Q: Do you know who did?

A: No, Sir.

Q: Do you know if anybody did?

A: I don't, but with all the criminals around; it wouldn't surprise me. Isn't that hard.

"Thank you, Mrs. Perkins. I have no further questions for this witness."

He thought it would be better to quit while he was behind with this fetching witness.

"You are excused, Mrs. Perkins," Judge Rotweillin said, "Call your next witness, Mr. Teitlebaum?"

"No, your Honor. The defense rests."

****

Ivory asked Damien for another favor. He was feeling desperate because he did not think the trial was going McGee's way.

"Look, Damien, I have got to talk to Victor Amuso or Al D'Arco to see if I can find out if they know if anybody from the Salerno and Aovese family in New York or even the Genoveses would know anything or might give us something for an adequate consideration."

"It's obvious you can't ask the Genoveses or the Salernos anything directly; so, maybe the godfather might see it as being in his best interest to do a little screw-over of the competition so long as neither him nor the Lucchese family appears to be involved. I'll give it a try.

Damien put the proposition to Victor Amuso who remained the official boss of the Lucchese crime family despite serving a bid in Sing-Sing for fraud; he was only doing a nickel and with time off for good behavior, he would be back in the city in less than a year. The conversation was via one of Amuso's contraband cell phones. To Damien's surprise, the don responded favorably.

"Damien, I like your work for us. I also like McGee and wouldn't mind doin' him a positive, especially if the Genoveses won't like it. You know, McGee did me personally a solid. The prison gangs came after me to make me pay a tax. Their ask was exorbitant. McGee and your friend Caitlin—a real smart broad—had a meet with somma the Blacks and Hispanics in the city and convinced them that it was in their best interests over all to play nice with me while I'm inside; so's business can go smooth among alla us on the outside. That McGee is a smooth talker. He don't deserve what's happenin' to him.

"Here's what I think oughta go down, and I'll grease the skids. You, and this Ivory guy, and Caitlin, take my acting boss Al D'Arco and Frank Lastorino. I don't think you know Big Frank. He's 84 years old but is still nobody to mess with. Besides, he knows were all the Genovese's bodies are buried. Frank "Big Frank" Lastorino is a made man. One time he was a capo and a former consigliere of the Lucchese family. He was formally inducted into the family in 1987, if memory serves me. I'll give 'em both a heads up and that I'd consider it a favor if they could help."

Damien said, "Don Victor, I can't imagine a better favor. Watch your back in there, okay?"

"Always, my man, always."

Ivory and Caitlin were elated. They pulled in a bunch of old markers and made reservations for eight [including the mob bosses' significant others] at Per Se, the French restaurant at No. 10 in The Shops at Columbus Circle. They reserved the VIP East Room for a Friday night for an extra king's ransom fee, and extra waiters imported from France. Only the best.

Ivory laughed when he got off the phone with the maître d, "I hope McGee's worth it. After all, he's a con. Who knows about those guys?"

Caitlin laughed at Ivory's intended irony since McGee had recently engineered a several hundred-million-dollar prison break for the firm's other con, Ivory White.

Ivory and Caitlin arrived early off 59th Street to check in early. He was wearing a black suit, silvery tie, and black shoes with best shine he had ever demanded from a shine boy. Caitlin had a new little black dress, a sequined black evening purse, black Gucci shoes with silver stiletto heels, a string of pearls and medium real pearl earrings. They met the maître d, Joseph Patrie-Sant Petit, although his height and powerful build belied the name. All was in readiness. They took a stroll around square and studied the statue of Christopher Columbus, for whom the square is named. It is a geographic center—the traditional municipal zero-mile point from which all official distances are calculated They found a lounge, sat down and waited half an hour for the mobsters and their molls to show up. The Per Se had excellent views of Central Park and Columbus Square; so the wait was very pleasant.

All the Lucchese bosses and their wives or girl-friends—including Damien and his new girlfriend,

Patrice Leathe—showed up on time and in proper dress—gentlemen must wear a jacket, and no jeans were allowed in the dining room. For women, a black cocktail dress is always a safe bet—which allayed Caitlin's fears.

Damien took care of the introductions and the order of seating: Caitlin next to Al D'Arco and his wife Maria-Innocenta; Ivory next to Frank Lastorino and his beautiful granddaughter, Francoise. Damien and Patrice took places among the rest of the Lucchese family elect. There were enough diamonds among the women to start their own fancy diamond mart.

The Per Se is Chef Keller's second three-Michelin-starred restaurant featuring a daily nine-course tasting menu and a nine-course vegetable tasting menu using classic French technique and the finest quality ingredients available (or imaginable). The wine list, boasted more than 2,000 bottles, including a collection of older wines as well as wines from small producers that were released only in limited quantities. The restaurant has the Grand Award from the *Wine Spectator*. It is not a discount place, even for large groups: $200 reservation fee per regular person, $400 each for the McGee Investigations party. The tips were expected to be commensurate.

The mobsters were used to cheap Italian cafes with spaghetti and beer. Per Se was a treat that called for a reciprocation. They knew that; nobody was duped. No business was mentioned during the entire meal; that would be when cigars and cognac were served to the men in the adjacent meeting room. For now, the five tuxedoed

waiters brought in the first course: pearl barley and por-
cini mushroom *Potage*; *creme fraiche "royale"*; brioche
croutons and celery branch ribbons; red wine braised
heirloom onions; *Ronde De Nice En Persillade*, and shirred
hen egg, for starters. The entrées included a platter with
a taste of several culinary extravaganzas like black truffle
and Beluga Caviar; *gougeres* [pastry stuffed with smooth
cheese aromatic cheese], salmon cones, which looked like
they weighed fifty pounds each. The cone had a wonder-
ful citrus flavor in the salmon and was heavy on the red
onion in the *creme fraiche* base.

The platters came in waves. The second wave held
oysters and pearls: "sabayon" of pearl tapioca with Island
Creek oysters and sterling white caviar–the signature Per
Se dish, where the main flavor is butter; and the main
texture is buttery; and the other main desire was the Pistachio Veneziana Hand Wrapped bread to sop it up with.
The subsequent waves included such unusual and marvel-
ous new dishes as *gateau* of Hudson valley moulard duck
foie gras; banana *Parisienne*; marinated sunchokes; pied-
mont hazelnuts, mizuna and tellicherry pepper yogurt;
strawberries and creme fraiche; pistachio and turnips;
and celery and leeks, included strawberries and creme
fraiche, pistachio and turnips, and celery and leeks,

The third platter was simple: a tasting of salts from
around the world to top the foie gras. The assortment
included pink Himalayan, black volcanic, and *fleur de sel*
salts. Next came platters of fillet of Atlantic halibut *confit a
la minute*, La Ratte potato coins, grilled artichokes, *piperade*,

parsley and squid ink ravigote; followed by butter poached Nova Scotia lobster; red wine braised radicchio; scarlet grapes; chestnut puré; *mâche* and smoked foie gras vinaigrette.

The final entrée platter held bacon wrapped Four Story Hill Farm's rabbit loin, heirloom carrots, cipollini onions, watercress and Hadley orchard's medjool date coulis; Snake River farms' *calotte de boeuf*; glazed short rib with crispy hen-of-the-woods mushrooms, petite radishes, wilted arrowleaf spinach and *sauce bordelaise*. To prepare the enthralled mobster gathering for dessert, they were served delicate Hass Avocado Sorbet; champagne mango sorbet; young coconut cream; and rambutan and coconut meringue to cleanse the palate.

These were hardy big men and excited women for whom the small mouthfuls of delicacies were not entirely enough. They still had enthusiasm for dessert. The platters of lavish choices were eye, nose, and brain, catching: chocolates of a dozen different flavors in 40 different shapes. They were molded, some of them truffles; there was fudge, and French macarons. The grandiose *de finale* was a three-tiered behemoth mountain of *mignardises*.

The meal ended with the ladies heading off to see a new movie—*Top Gun: Maverick*–in an exclusive pre-release showing in the luxurious Cinépolis Luxury Cinema. They turned down the free popcorn. The men made an immediate metamorphosis into hard talking, hard bargaining, completely objective, businessmen whose business was crime.

Acting Lucchese boss, D'Arco opened the business meeting with no idle nattering, "Damien and Ivory, that was a great meal. Thanks. You softened us up for the touch. What is it, exactly?"

Damien spoke for Ivory and Caitlin, "Our good friend—who you guys know well—needs serious help. He is in Rikers on a bum charge, and his trial looks like it's not gonna end in his favor. We need an edge, a big one. What we think would do the trick is for some Genovese soldier or capo to get arrested by one of New York's finest who is friendly to the Luccheses. It will need to be for something real, something that would put him away for a "day and a night". The cops will have to wring outta him a deal to turn in whoever in the Genovese Family did the actual killings in return for a light sentence and some dough. I'm sure you all can come up with a patsy; the question is, will you?"

"Not to crass or overly mercenary, but what's in it for us, Damien?"

"A million bucks each… and a good dinner, no haggling."

D'Arco laughed, "I like your approach, Damien. How about we vote? You can have a vote along with us; you're part of the family."

The vote required no negotiation. It was unanimous in Damien and the McGee Investigations, Inc. visitors' favor.

Caitlin said to Ivory on the way home, "That was some very expensive rice, Emperor's rice."

"And worth every penny."

Chapter Fifteen

The Summary

Judge Rotweillin called the court to order and proceeded directly to explain in detail the legal actions of a criminal case and federal criminal court procedures, the responsibilities of all participants, including the jurors, and what was going to happen next. He stressed the great importance of the concept of "guilt beyond a reasonable doubt" and emphasized that it was not "beyond the shadow of a doubt", nor was it a mere preponderance of evidence as in a civil trial.

"Now, here is something you could possibly think is unfair. Let me instruct you regarding Rule 29.1 in the Federal Rules of Criminal Procedure: Under the Sixth Amendment to the Constitution, defendants have a right to present a defense. They are also entitled to give a closing argument but are not required to do so. In this court, the prosecution **first** makes a closing argument, then the defense attorney. The prosecutor, who has the burden of proof–not the defendant–has the chance to respond—called a rebuttal–to the defense's final argument. Because the prosecution has the burden of proof, it gets the final word. Both sides have the opportunity to argue to the jury why it should find in their favor. Listen to those arguments but withhold judgment until both sides have had their say."

He made the pro forma request at this juncture if the lawyers had any further trial motions.

Equally pro forma, Defense Attorney Yitzack Teitlebaum rose, and said, "Motion of Motion for judgment of acquittal, your Honor."

Deputy US Attorney Franklin Caruthers rose and made the counter motion, "The prosecution asks, on what grounds?"

Teitleman answered, "Insufficient evidence."

In two seconds, his Honor ruled, "Denied."

He then asked the prosecution and defense if they were ready to give their summations. Both men answered that they were.

"Proceed for the prosecution."

Caruthers stood in front of the jury holding a blue ring binder from which he read from time to time. He followed the general rules of a proper closing argument to the letter: A recitation of what the evidence showed: a down pat clear and concise description of the laws that apply in the case; An illustration of how the law applied to the facts proven—most particularly the fingerprint finding and identification of McGee's prints as being a match. He stated the reasons why the facts did not support the other side's position, namely, they did not present evidence just supposition, however learned and clever the witnesses for the defense. He repeated the most pertinent portions of the judge's jury instructions and a reminder to the jury that they must follow them. He urged them to remember, the evidence does not have to be perfect—only beyond a *reasonable* doubt.

"Ladies and Gentlemen of the jury, if you pay close attention to both the evidence and the law, you are duty bound to find Mr. McGee guilty as charged. Thank you for your service."

Mr. Teitlebaum stood up as soon as Caruthers settled into his seat by the prosecution desk.

"Ladies and Gentlemen of the jury, thanks for lasting through this trial. I know it has been tedious at times, but I am sure you are well aware that a man's life is at stake here. What you do and decide is important. Mr. Caruthers gave a fine summation; I am sure you will agree. However–as you might expect–I have to hold up my hand and say, "Hey, not so fast."

"He left a few things out. The only real evidence in this trial is the finding of Mr. McGee's fingerprints at the crime scenes... plural. How did they get there? Unknown and unproved. They were so very clear and precise, both sides' experts commented that they were "perfect", perhaps too much so. In fact, it is rare to see such perfect prints–let alone two exactly matching ones–in two different crime scenes. How much weight should you give to the fingerprint evidence? A wag once said, 'it don't matter what you know, if what you know ain't so.'

"Our defense witnesses—one a remarkable expert, and one a regular citizen—showed clearly how prints can be faked. It is not that hard, and the transfer of bogus prints is not at all difficult. No schooling required, unless you think 'criminal tutelage' counts. The US government has cautioned us to be wary of fingerprint evidence; and I, for one, think there is something rotten in Denmark; and the prosecution should never have proffered them as evidence.

"I won't belabor my points. The facts... the actual provable facts, are skimpy, and this fingerprint evidence is not enough to convict. There is reasonable doubt, and you are reasonable people. Think what you have seen and heard, then do the right thing. Vote unanimously to acquit. Thank you."

The rebuttal was brief to the point of being terse.

"The prosecution does not have to prove motive or extenuating circumstances. Mr. McGee's fingerprints were found on both murder weapons; about that, there is no argument. He is guilty of premeditated first-degree multiple murders and must be found guilty; so, he cannot ever again perpetrate such heinous crimes. Let your minds and your consciences be your guides."

"The jury is excused to begin its deliberations," the judge said, "Court is adjourned until they return."

He banged his gavel.

CHAPTER SIXTEEN

OTHER CRIMES AND MISDEMEANORS

The McGee trial was being covered in detail in *the New York Times* and on CNN; so, Six Fingers was more or less keeping up. He read that the jury was out, and the verdict was coming soon, not that he cared all that much. McGee would get his comeuppance if he was sent to any New York prison where the mafia had a strong presence. Learn who not to disrespect. Speaking of that, it seemed Don Guillermo "Barney" Trafficante, the boss, was giving him the cold shoulder lately; and that could not be good. He needed to impress the boss, and the opportunity to shine just dropped in his lap. It seems that the Genoveses set up a casino on 116th Street—which had become firmly part of Lucchese territory after the former capo went to prison on RICO charges. That was unacceptable. The Genoveses were the interlopers, and they had to go.

Otto "Six-Fingers" Castellammarese–number two in the Genovese Family at the time–decided to act without going through the boss to demonstrate his power and service. He was determined to effect a change in ownership of the casino which left him holding the reins of power. It was risky, but he needed the creds. He met with Terry "The Undertaker" Esposito in the Battaglia Brothers Café in the Bronx during an off-hours opportunity.

"How's it hangin' Ter?" Six-Fingers asked.

"Good. Long time no see my man, what's up?"

"Why does somethin' always have to be up? Maybe I was just in the 'hood and happened by."

Terry laughed.

"A bit outta your comfort zone over here, aren't ya, boss?"

"Maybe. Or maybe I got some business to take care of."

"What kinda business, "Six-fingers? And does it involve me and crew, I'd bet?"

"Funny you'd use that word… bet. Actually, has somethin' to do with bettin'. You heard about the Lucchess's tryin' to take back the 116th street casino again?"

"Some. Heard a new capo… name a… Carmine, somethin'. But ain't he one a us Genoveses?"

"Right, Carmine Giuffrida, come over from Palermo."

"Old mustache Pete?"

"Family is. He's got a fancy-samancy education, finance or somethin'."

"It's a new world, boss."

"Not so new; he's ambitious; and he can poach in our territory, Undertaker. I want you to take a look, a hard one, if ya get my meanin'."

"Ya want he should swim with the fishes?"

"Glad you axed. Not wet work, this time. We want ta feed him to the cops; we have bigger fish to fry."

"Will my help be appreciated?"

"You know it will. Don't I always?"

"That you do. Gimme the particulars then. I'll take care of it."

Two COs came onto the unit and marched directly to McGee's house. He was taking a nap at the time, and they rudely woke him up.

"Rise and shine Number NYPD 10451-05222022 FEL-M,1, we gotta get you back to the courtroom, PDQ."

The process was now routine. He was handcuffed at the wrists, shackled at the ankles; and both sets of restraints were attached to a waist shackle. They shuffled him along the corridors cheered on by a choir of hoots and hollers, most of which was friendly and well-wishing.

He was placed in his seat at the defense table in the court room. The bailiff gave the "all-rise" order, and Judge Rotweillin strode to his raised bench and bade all to resume their seats.

"Bring in the jury."

The 12 impaneled jury members and two alternates took their seats. Most of the jurors looked glum, and Mr. Teitlebaum tried to hide his disappointment from McGee. One of the jurors, number 8, could scarcely contain the smile that kept breaking out. McGee was aware that he was the one juror who had fixed his gaze on him and retained a malevolent glare until today, whatever that meant.

"Madam foreperson, have you reached a verdict?"

"We have," and she handed the folded jury verdict sheet to the bailiff who delivered into the hands of the judge. He glanced at it briefly, and handed it back to the bailiff, who returned it to the foreperson.

There was a moment of hush and anxiety in the room.

"How do you find?" Judge Rotrweillin asked with a practiced lack of emotion.

The foreperson gave a little cough to clear her throat.

McGee was afraid his poor heart was going to jump out of his chest.

"For the crime of multiple murder in the first degree, we find the defendant, JPAMJ McGee guilty."

The courtroom erupted into a yelling, shuffling, hurrying, mob, the members of which—mostly reporters—could not move fast enough to exit and get their stories out to the waiting public. McGee was hustled back to the jail and found himself alone in his cell. The guards had housed his cellie in another unit for the night.

The following day, the same transfer back to the court was repeated. It was sentencing day, and the time when the angry and bereaved families could vent their spleens at the murderer who had taken their loved ones.

The prosecutor demanded execution. Mr. Teitle-baum argued vehemently for the lesser sentence of life without parole, the only real option he had. The family members for all five victims took their opportunity to castigate the monster who had murdered the innocents in cold blood and without remorse. They, too, demanded the death penalty.

The following day… late afternoon, McGee was returned to the court to hear his sentence.

Judge Rotrweillin was dressed all in black as was juror number 8, oddly enough.

"I have pondered overnight about this verdict. It is the most difficult decision I ever have to make. Given the heinous quality of these murders and the lack of remorse on the part of the convict JPAMJ McGee, I am compelled to order the maximum, execution.

"Mr. McGee you have taken the lives of nine human beings, all innocents. You have stolen the joy and pleasure of association of these families with their loved ones forever. Perhaps you can reflect on that as you await execution. May God have mercy on your soul."

He banged his gavel extra hard; and two prison guards stood McGee up, shackled him, and shoved him roughly out of the courtroom, out of the hall, out of the courthouse, and into the drab prison van with heavy wire on the windows. He was roughly pushed into his new cell and in all likelihood, his last one... death row, number five.

CHAPTER SEVENTEEN

APPEAL

The level of shock among McGee's friends and lawyers was incalculable both for the verdict and the extreme harshness of the sentence. The news media had a field day extravaganza of hyperbole, analysis, and excess, which created considerable income for the industry. So-called experts—talking heads–flooded the television channels, blogs, and newspaper, accounts. McGee himself disappeared from all outside media. In fact, he was removed from New York. Federally death sentenced prisoners are housed in only two BOP [Bureau of Prisons] facilities: Male prisoners are incarcerated in the SCU [Special Confinement Unit] at the United States Penitentiary in Terre Haute, Indiana. Three days after his sentencing, McGee was transferred there in the middle of the night. Only his attorney-of-record, Yitzack Teitleman was notified.

At SCU Terre Haute, death row inmates are kept in a cell 6 feet by 9 feet by 9.5 feet high. Currently, there were forty-sex men on Death Row.

The death row guard who pushed him into the recently vacated cell told him two things: "This cell used to be home to Ray Bradcliff, the torture murderer of twenty-six people. He occupied it until about two weeks ago when they transferred him to the small cell. FYI, when a new death row inmate–such as yourself–arrives, he gets this big cell. When a death warrant is signed, the inmate is moved to a cell 7 feet by 12 feet by 8.5 feet high. Life as a man awaiting execution had begun for McGee.

Later in the afternoon, the row's shift guard stood in front of McGee's cell.

"You got a important visitor… lawyer."

"Well, please show him into my parlor," McGee said.

"My pleasure," the guard said, and the two of them shared a brief laugh.

He expected to see Yitzach Teitleman enter the door with the guard; but instead, the guard escorted a fiftyish tanned gentleman with greying sideburns and temple hair. He was tall, fit, and tanned, and he was wearing a custom fitted charcoal grey suit, University of Virginia black tie with an orange image of Monticello on it. He wore gleaming black shoes and a friendly, honest smile.

"We'll need the attorney interview room," he said to the guard.

"He'll have to be shackled," the guard pointed out.

"Not when he's in the room with me. And, we will require absolute privacy, even electronic."

"Of course."

McGee was required to stand with his face to the wall of his cell and be shackled hand, foot, and waist. Two guards escorted him and his potential new lawyer to the interview room. He was seated, unshackled, then allowed to speak to the attorney. There were two-way mirrors on all walls, but no sound transmission.

"Nice digs, you have here."

"Thanks."

"Have you settled in okay?"

"Okay."

"Are you being treated decently?"

"Yeah."

"The judge assigned my firm to represent you because this is a capital case. Your Mr. Teitlebaum was all right[but he was up against a block wall of prosecutors, biased cops, and, frankly, a biased judge. I will explain all that later. For now, just know a pertinent established fact: Judicial system reviews reveal that capital court cases in the US—federal and state–are often biased, arbitrary, and error prone.

"In your case, I think your entire experience demonstrated all three. In an opinion, legal experts have blasted as "nightmarish" and "an abomination," the US Supreme Court has ruled in two Arizona death penalty cases that 1990s amendments to the federal habeas corpus law permit state prisoners who were provided ineffective representation at trial and in post-conviction proceed-ings to argue that their counsel were ineffective but bar them from presenting evidence of their ineffectiveness that competent lawyers had discovered once the case had reached federal court.

"We are up against such bias, but that is the world where we work. Both state and federal law require repre-sentation of death row inmates by proven and certified law firms with significant experience in the complicated and difficult process, and firms that have shown that they can stay the duration.

"You have the right to select your own attorney; but, I suggest that you do not have the expertise to do so. You can take time–make changes or not–but do not do so on the basis of any kind of emotional bias. It's kind of a crap shoot for prisoners who lack funds, but my preliminary investigations indicates that you have sufficient to see the expensive process all the way through. Anything to say or ask, McGee?"

"Not really. I think it is probably important to get going quickly and in strength. I am sure you are alto-gether competent which is one strike in my favor. The other is that my partners are major investigators and very good at what they do. I suggest that you use them and their ideas for fact finding, even knowing that they are not lawyers. This is probably impulsive, but let's get going. Where do I sign?"

"I just so happen to have documents here for you to sign. Incidentally, I am the Blackwell—Stephen

Blackwell–of Blackwell, Sternberg, and Dastrup. I will be in touch on a regular basis, and I will probably be able to have the documents for appeal to the United States Second Circuit in the Thurgood Marshall US Courthouse in New York by the end of the week.

"Thanks."

McGee's deep grey mood was beginning to lighten up.

Caitlin O'Brian received a telephone call on her mobile phone at about the same time as McGee was talking to his new attorney.

"Hello, is this Caitlin O'Brian?"

"It is."

"This is the White House. Will you accept a call from the President of the United States?"

"Certainly."

"Hello, is this Caitlin, associate of McGee and Ivory?"

"The same."

"This is President Sybil Norcroft Daniels. How are you holding up?"

"As good as can be expected, Madam President. It has been a terrible time."

"I can only imagine. I have been wracking my brain trying to come up with a way to help McGee. Any ideas for me?"

"Ivory and I have been doing the same thing and have a few irons in the fire, but nothing has clicked so far. With all your power and influence, there must be something that you could come up with—use your intelligence networks, just your influence, maybe."

"I can't really do any of that, short of actually trumping something phony up. That would almost certainly screw him up all the more. I do have one final legal thing I can do, and that is to grant him a pardon. I think it would be better to wait to see if we can get a real innocent final verdict. I'll do it as a last resort because I believe in the man."

"Thank you, Madam President. We are certain that he's been framed. It was neatly done, and we are banging our heads against a wall trying to find proof. We will keep you in the loop."

"Good. Maybe I can send him some cookies."

"Probably better to use a fake name and address, Ma'am."

That lightened the mood before they disconnected.

The Second Circuit Appeals Court received the application for a hearing two weeks later. It did not take them long to decline—on the basis that they would only grant a hearing if there was new evidence. Stephen Blackwell was not the least bit surprised, and he had no good piece of evidence. He decided to give McGee's partners a call to see if they had anything.

The firm's receptionist answered, "McGee and Associates, how may I direct your call?"

"Hello. This is Stephen Blackwell, I am Mr. McGee's new attorney. May I speak to either or both Caitlin or Ivory?"

"I'll have both on the line in a jiffy. Do you mind holding for a minute?"

"Not at all."

It was only a little more than a minute. Both partners connected.

"Hello, Mr. Blackwell, we are on a conference call line."

"First, let's be on a first name basis. We are going to be talking frequently, I reckon."

"Fine. What's up, Stephen?"

"The Second Circuit Appeal was denied. I did not have evidence of a specific error from the district court. I have read the entire transcript, and I am sure the fingerprint evidence was planted, and I am equally sure that not enough effort was put looking into it, but I can't prove it."

"We agree 100%, and that is where we are looking."

"I have my own investigator. She is great. Mind if she gets read in? The three of you should be able to work together smoothly and efficiently. She is easy to work with and has a lot of street smarts. Name's Alice Mary Craig."

"Send her over. We'll take any help we can get."

It was eleven p.m., time to open the 116th street casino for business. There was a discrete queue gathering in the enclosed anteroom waiting for the opportunity to throw away their money. Genovese Family Capo Carmine Giuffrida had on his sharp new tuxedo and a bright shark's smile.

"Welcome, welcome," he greeted each new sucker and ushered them into the newly redecorated gambling parlor.

Each man—and three women—had been thoroughly vetted before being told when and where to come for a night of fun on the wild side.

Not thoroughly enough: two of the twenty-two gamblers were undercover detectives from the CEU [Civil Enforcement Unit], and another from the Lucchese family had clandestinely made the cut. The CEU uses civil litigation in both judicial and administrative venues to expand the NYPD's ability to respond to crimes. Attorneys work with law enforcement personnel to address pervasive ongoing criminal organizations and conditions, such as: illegal firearms, DUI, narcotics, prostitution, weapons, trademark counterfeiting, auto crime, and—in this case, gambling. Neither cops nor Luccheses were aware of the presence of each other. There were a few well-known faces—a city council man from Harlem, a ranking NYPD officer, and two famous Broadway actors, one male and one female—in the group.

Scantily clad young beauties escorted the high rollers to their assigned seats at the six-sided poker tables. Roulette and craps were available as restful alternatives for the sweaty work of poker. Once everyone was accounted for and seated, the well-known mistress of New York's underground gambling walked into the room wearing her signature scarlet silk full length gown and necklace of rubies strung on red string. The necklace framed her ample decolletage framing it in a thorough attention getting fashion.

"Good evening, ladies and gentlemen, friends now and perhaps foes later in the evening."

Everyone laughed knowing full well how things were going to go. Six burly bouncers were strategically placed to ensure that things did not go too far.

"For our newcomers, I'll recite the rules of play. For the old timers, be patient."

She listed six cardinal rules: No fighting, no yelling, no long sleeves, no smoking or spitting tobacco, no drinking to excess–the definition of that left up to "Big Red" as she was known to everyone.

"Cheaters—no matter how important you think you are—will get a trip to the woodshed with our nice bouncers. Let's not have any of that. Now, let's begin. First game is Texas hold'em. Ante is $50,000, no counterfeit dough allowed."

That brought a good general laugh.

Everyone received a tumbler of well-aged cognac to soften them up and depress their intellects, and the games began.

Quitting time was 0200, and the game fervor was beginning to lag. Suddenly the front and rear doors of the casino burst open and in charged a dozen combat-clad NYPD SWAT team members shouting and shoving.

"ON THE FLOOR, POLICE!; ON THE FLOOR; HANDS WHERE WE CAN SEE THEM!!!"

The obedience was grudging but prompt. Carmine Giuffrida tried to slither towards the security of his lockable office, but two cops pinned him to the floor and cuffed him.

Every person in the place: bouncers, dealers, spotters, and gamblers, was cuffed with his or her hands behind their backs and did a perp walk out the front door of the building into a klieg light glare of police and media lights. The newspaper reporters, photogs, and TV crews, flashed camera stills and videos for the eleven o'clock news and tomorrow's headlines on the newspapers. Reporters shouted names and demanded responses, but the heads-down members of the perp walk clammed up tightly.

A convoy of paddy wagons filled front to back and side to side with furious rich gamblers wove its way through the Bronx streets to the NYPD 25th Precinct Station house situated less than 800 feet from the local 116th Street station on the IRT Lexington Avenue Line of the New York City Subway. The lucky gambling aficionados and helpmeets were treated to a second all-out perp walk into the precinct building. Every man and woman was assigned an AO, read his/her Miranda rights, and shoved and pushed into a twenty person holding cell. There were twenty-eight of them in all.

In no particular order, each participant was called out and arrangements were made for them to be hauled to the Tombs for central booking, no privileges granted.

Genovese Family Capo Carmine Giuffrida, was the 13th person to be selected for the opportunity.

"Can't we talk reason?" he muttered to his bulky attendants.

"Sure can, right this way."

Out of sight of everyone else, he was taken to an interview room on the floor above.

"Have a seat, Carmine... mind if I call you Carmine?" Manhattan Homicide Bureau detective, Kyle Ritchens, D. 1, asked courteously.

His partner, Abigail "Abby" Maartens D. III, wore a soda cracker expression throughout.

"Nope. Call me what youse wants."

"We're going to have to study your RAP sheet before we have our talk, Carmine. Chill out and think carefully about what we might have to say."

They let him squirm an hour and a half before returning.

"Sorry about the wait, Carmine. Busy night, as you might have noticed."

"I noticed. Let's get down to brass tacks, how about?"

"Good, I like the efficiency of that plan. My partner and I will have to help send a fair number of perps to the can tonight to do our share."

Abigail took the questioner's role.

"Carmine, you can call me Detective Third. We have read over your sheet; quite impressive. In fact, if we do the math right, you qualify as a third time loser for this tag. Puts you at a real disadvantage. Anything you would like to contribute before we set in motion your new home as Sing-Sing?"

"Nope. My lips is zipped."

"Too bad that a young guy like you will get life for this one. Your four kids are going to be sad without a father, don't you think? And—by the way—your house is being searched with a warrant as we speak. We have evidence to suggest that your sweet wife, Angelina, may be mixed up in your business as well. It would be really sad if your kids suddenly became orphans."

"Youse'll never make it stick. My mouthpiece'll have me outta here before breakfast. Youse are gointa regret this. Ya don't know who yer messin' with. Ask around, then come back; and we'll see how our little parlay goes."

"Not a lot of time tonight, Carmine. We interpret one of your recorded utterances to be the preliminary to an offer of bribery. That ups the ante seriously."

"Lawyer." Carmine said with a surly grin.

"See what we can do, Bro," said Richens.

"Youse do that. Make it pronto. I gotta headache."

They let him stew in the little room with no air-conditioning on an uncomfortable metal chair, hands cuffed to a bar in front of him for another hour and a half.

He was squirming when the two detectives returned.

"My butt hurts. This is police brutality. I'm gonna sue. Where's my lawyer?" he snarled.

"It pains me to report that we have not been able to locate the man," Abigail said deadpan.

"And youse tried real hard."

"Of course. And, oh, we have some news to report. You know Tony "the nose", Carmine?"

"Course I do; he'onna the bouncers."

"Actually, he is one of Don Guillermo "Barney" Trafficante's top dogs unbeknownst to you. He is one of the top three made men who controls gambling in the five boroughs and Chicago. Tony has decided to work for us for a while. His first offer was you. He says you paid off juror number eight in the McGee trial. That ring a bell, Carmine?"

Carmine did not speak.

"He did, and you know it. Otherwise, how would we come up with such a thing? He will testify against you in open court, and that will be the last nail in your coffin. Tony says, Barney will stay out of it, because he has no intention of becoming incriminated. You are on your own, Carmine. It doesn't look good."

Carmine was quiet for a few minutes, his face a mask of intense concentration.

Finally, he asked, "What's in it for me, if I turn state's evidence with some juicy stuff, Detectives?"

"Depends on the 'stuff', but if you give us important stuff, we can get these charges dropped, and you won't be a three-time loser. Of course, you'll have to be a snitch for us for the rest of your natural life."

"What do I get if a drop a dime on say… Otto "Six-Fingers" of the Genoveses?"

"Make it good, and we'll get you full immunity and into WITSEC right after you testify."

"Me and my family, too?"

"Yes, and with enough money to get a head start in a decent place. The practice of trading information for guilt is so common that it has literally become a thriving business, Carmine; and we are experts at this kind of business."

"Awright, let's talk bidness."

CHAPTER EIGHTEEN

MEETINGS BETWEEN ANGEL AND DEVILS

S tephen Blackwell was the first to get the news from the 25th precinct about Carmine Giuffrida caving in and the information he promised to share even in court. He let the McGee partners know and suggested that they meet. Ivory asked that they be allowed to include Damien Markee. Stephen was reluctant but allowed himself to be persuaded when he heard Ivory's plan.

The meeting took place in lower Harlem at the home of one of Ivory's old homies. They sat in the living room in a semi-circle and listened to Attorney Blackwell's communication.

"Lead detective Kyle Ritchens, D. 1, was the AO who handled Carmine Giuffrida. I don't know if you ever heard of him. He was the manager of the Genovese casino on 116th Street in the Bronx until two weeks ago when NYPD staged a quick and dirty raid. It made the news, and a lot of prominent names came up. For our purposes, the only one that matters is this Giuffrida gangster. He caved and coped to a plea in which he got off from the gambling charge and probable 3-time loser status. That would have put him in hard time for life. He gave full details about who ordered the jury tampering, why, and how Giuffrida did it—money that changed hands, communications; and how the juror–a man named Gino Poletti–talked the jury into a guilty verdict. Giuffrida got WITSEC and will disappear into it after he testifies in open court."

Everyone in the room stared at Blackwell, dumb founded–too shocked to be sure that McGee would surely have his verdict nullified by the judge.

"So, tell us the details, Stephen," Damien urged. "We have to know where this could go wrong. Call me the pessimist in the room."

"Sure, this is the short version: Carmine said one of the bailiffs, name of Doug Gabler, was in the Genovese's pocket. He called Carmine and told him he knew one of the jurors in the McGee case, and he knew him well enough to know he could be bought. He told Carmine that juror eight had three things going for him; he was strapped for cash; he had a secret history of doing some heavy work for the Genoveses back in the day; and he had a second cousin who was put in jail by McGee's work in a case of kidnapping that took place in Redhook—Saint Anne's Mother of Mary Orphanage. McGee and Associates was heavily involved in bringing the girls back home.

"All it took was a phone call, one brief meeting, a transfer of half of the agreed upon bribe; and the juror number eight, Jack Gino Poletti, was agreeable. Polette earned his money. He spent hours unflinchingly arguing in favor of a guilty verdict, and again for the death penalty. Now, get this, who do you think gave Poletti his final payment?"

"Carmine," Caitlin said,

"Most likely answer, but wrong. It was the Genovese don himself, Don Guillermo "Barney" Trafficante."

"Why on earth would he do that?"

"Seems Barney wanted the guy to come and work for the Genoveses and wanted him to know who was the boss."

"Those guys never cease to amaze me. That would leave the don open to being outed. So, is he the killer... seems unlike him?"

"He said 'no' and Richens believes him. I'm not sure. But, apparently, Barney was being cagey, he knew the fibbies were after him on RICO charges, and he obliquely asked about the possibility of being granted immunity. He wouldn't say anymore but hinted that there could be more on another day if the FBI got too close. He suggested that doing a long stretch in stir was not for him; it was just for the little people."

"What happens next?"

"I do my best to get the case back into District Judge Hyman Rotweillin's court to get him to nullify the verdict, or at least grant a new trial."

"Sounds like a slam dunk," Ivory said, "so, what's the catch?"

Stephen laughed.

"Bellomo hinted about Castellammareser but was cagey to the end. We will probably have to start on the level of the prosecutor and work our way back into court. Both the prosecutor and the judge have a vested interest in ignoring the evidence. The guilty verdict and the harsh sentence looks good on both their records. Rotweillin wants to retire with a conspicuous win and the ambitious prosecutors–attorneys general for the SDNY–Milton Weilenbach and Deputy Franklin Caruthers–are looking ahead to elevation to the DOJ even to be the Attorney General or to get a judgeship eventually, to one of the 13 Courts of Appeals–intermediate appellate courts— benches–and beyond, one day."

"You can never discount ambition in government," observed Damien, speaking for the first time.

"No, you can't, and we will have to tread lightly."

CHAPTER NINETEEN

RETRIAL?

M r. Blackwell sent a formal request to Judge Rotweillin with full details of recent developments. He offered the opinion that this was different than an attempt to introduce new evidence of McGee's innocence, but rather, that this was indicative of an administrative cause for a review in the appellate court. It—in no way—cast doubt on the Judge's behavior or even that of the prosecution, or on any witnesses. The communication was not quite obsequious, but it was very carefully framed so as not to offend. Blackwell avoided even a tiny hint of motives of ambition on anyone's part. The Judge replied that he would not stand in the way of McGee's appeal, nor would he make a recommendation.

The death row attorney reapplied to the Second Circuit for a hearing on the administrative basis and was very pleasantly surprised to receive an appointment to make his appeal with a limit of 15 minutes for both sides.

He studied every scintilla of evidence he could gather in order to present a cogent and persuasive argument for either a vacation of the judgment or a referral back to the federal district court of origin. He planned to be assertive because he believed both as a defense attorney in the law and as an educated and experienced person that the established charge of jury tampering was reason enough. He practiced his body and face movements before the mirror and had his wife clock him multiple times; so, he would not go over his allotted time.

On the day, SDNY Chief US Attorney Milton Weilenbach used up his time stating the obvious: McGee's fingerprints were on the murder weapons, and no one contests that fact. Blackwell avoided even the mention of evidence and concentrated on telling a convincing rendition of the jury tampering. He had left himself sufficient time to assert with vigor that the new information required the appellate court either to vacate the verdict or to order a new trial.

It took three weeks for the Second Circuit to respond; the ruling was terse: "The Federal District Court of the Southern District of New York, shall retry the case of United States v. JPAMJ McGee."

Owing to the depression over his experience with the justice system thus far, McGee did not permit himself to leap for joy. He did thank his new lawyer for his well-thought-out appeal and for winning it. He did not relish a rehash of the trial. Judge Rotweillin and the prosecutors were furious and determined to have a repeat of the guilty verdict that would—in all probability be the figurative final nail in McGee's coffin—and would accrue public and private kudos for their work. Blackwell met with every past witness, Mr. Teitlebaum and his staff, and McGee—multiple times—as well as all but memorizing the trial transcript. It was his practice and would be demonstrated once again in this retrial that he did not use notes and that what he said came from his heart as well as his experienced intellect.

While the legal machinations were winding their way through the court system, Caitlin, Ivory, and new temporary partners in the project—Damien and Alice Mary Craig, Blackwell's investigator—were pursuing an unsub who was the actual murderer. At least in their opinion, but it was now an idee fixe in each of their minds. Cops were of no help, no even Caitlin's friend, Detective Sergeant Emily "Em" Conraad who would be a contributor if she had anything to contribute. Damien's gang contacts had to ask questions very carefully, and on the down-low, lest their inquiries reach the upper echelons of the Luccheses who would clap a lid on all talk about the subject with their guys, including their cops, and the teamsters.

Alice Mary had an in with the teamsters from when she had investigated a supposed mob killing by one of the trustees. Working with the rank-and-file, they had turned up exculpatory evidence that resulted in the accused being set free. Teamsters have long memories about things like that. The union's general presidency office was vacant with the death of Henry Lythgoe—just an acting president–and the general secretary-treasurer, Otto "Six-Fingers" Castellammarese, was the main person to be kept in the dark. The clandestine investigators had to concentrate on the 22 vice-presidents and three trustees who served as watchdogs over the international union's finances.

Alice Mary's dogged persistence paid off. One of the trustees, Elmer Gorton, had been elected from the ranks a year before. His entire adult life, he had been a long-haul semi-truck driver; and he had the honest straight forward sense of right and wrong that characterized blue collar workers all around the world. He was sick and tired of the criminal shenanigans and domination of his union by the Genovese Family. His level of pique about the big guys was about to boil over, and Alice Mary caught him on a day when he was ready to vent his spleen.

Alice Mary was walking around in the truck repair shed of the ABF Freight System-Chapel Hill, on 153 Red Lion Road, Southampton, New Jersey when she overheard Gorton ventilating to the local teamster's boss, Giles Carnegie.

Gorton said, "Look, Giles, I don't mind a little corner cuttin' now and then in favor of the union. And I don't care over much that the presidents, general secretary-treasurers take a little cut, but if somebody don't do somethin' about the murders PDQ, then I'm gonna just take my pension and move to Florida."

"You talkin' about the New York dame… what was her name… who got hacked to pieces a while ago, Elmer?"

"That's the latest and worst, yeah. Her name was some funny French one… oh, yeah, it was Toussaint, I think."

"But, what can the likes of us nobuddies do about anthin' like that. It would be like accusin' God of a crime."

"I know. But someday, somebody has to do somethin', and it has to be from within the union or the feds will do it for us, mark my words."

"Well, it would have to be on the QT or else the whistle blower would get a cement suit for the annual union outing."

Gorton was still steamed up when Alice Mary Craig accidentally on purpose ran into him.

"Hey, Elmer, sorry about that. Look I couldn't help hearing what you and Giles Carnegie were talking about. It's not exactly my business, but maybe I can help. I can get something done on the DL without anybody knowing it came from you. And I'm not a cop. I'm a PI."

"Like what? And I didn't git yer name."

"Name's Alice Mary Craig, glad to meet you," Alice Mary said and extended her work hardened hand.

They shook.

"For some reason, I feel like trustin' you. I am sick of the criminal control over alla the good guys in the teamsters. Let's find a spot to have a talk."

They found a cluttered storeroom with boxes to sit on.

"What do you wanna know, specifically?"

"Who killed Lythgoe and his wife and the Toussaint woman, why, and how. And, is there any evidence or witnesses that could make the case in court?"

"I'll tell you this, I am willing to take my chances and testify against Six Fingers in the Lythgoe case. He asked me to find a hitman who could do a job and keep any information outta the press and even from the Geneveses. I told him "no" but that I would keep my mouth shut. Would that help?"

"Might. Anything else?"

"It is common knowledge among the higher-ups that Six Fingers had a thing goin' with that Toussaint floozy. He was keepin' her in that swanky penthouse, like she was his pet monkey. Apparently, there were a few young, better lookin' guys who wanted to horn in, and Fingers didn't like that. He passed the word that if anybody messed with her, they'd be fish food. That scared most of them off. But, I know she told him he wasn't able to do the job, if you get my meanin'.

"Anyways, one evening after an opera, the two had a big row right in the lobby in front of a whole bunch of hotel employees who were in the middle of change-of-shift. She hollered right out loud that he needed something stronger than Viagra, and there were men in her life that didn't need it at all. He hauled of and hit her on the side of her neck with a backhand and clocked her. He made the workin' stiffs haul her up to her bedroom where he dumped her. He threatened everyone who saw or heard anything with bein' torture murdered if they breathed a word. Nobody has so far as I know"

"It is likely to be called 'hearsay', but would you add that to your court testimony?"

"Yeah. Maybe you oughta give a thought about puttin' me and the missus into witness protection, if it comes to that, whatta you think?"

"Look, Elmer, I don't get any say in that kinda decision, but I will pass it on to my lawyer. He's a tough bugger who is able to work the system real well. I think you will likely get your say."

"Okay, that's good enough for me. I am not about to say nothin' about this, and I hope you're the same kinda person Mary Alice."

"Elmer, it would do nothing but hurt my lawyer and the client; and it would help our mutual pal, Otto "Six-Fingers" Castellammarese get away with murder. If I were a teamster, I would start worrying about when my number was up."

CHAPTER TWENTY

GRUDGING RETRIAL WITH JUDGE ROTWEILLIN PRESIDING

Pretrial motions and arguments where the most important aspects of the new trial of US v. McGee, but the transcriptions were sealed by order of the judge. All appearances were that this would just be a replay of the previous trial, except that the crooked juror would not be present; he was awaiting his own trial. The other change was that Yitzack Teitlebaum would not be sitting at the defense bench. He was on the defense witness list. The new defense was a team of three attorneys, all from the firm of Blackwell, Sternberg, and Dastrup. They were as well dressed and looked every bit as confident as the US Attorneys, Weilenbach and Caruthers seated near the jury box behind the prosecution table.

As it turned out, voir dire for jury selection took longer than the actual trial.

"Are you ready to proceed, Mr. Weilenbach?" the judge asked.

"May it please the court, we have come into new evidence that may be exculpatory for the defendant; so, it is our request that your Honor enter a judgment that nullifies the jury's verdict in the last trial, and seek to have the Supreme Court grant a writ of certiorari as to whether that can or should be done, and whether a second trial be commenced. Given the lengthy time this trial has been in the process of adjudication, we ask that the certiorari pleading be placed on an urgent track."

"Anything from the defense, Mr. Blackwell?"

"We agree with the plea and with the urgency. Who is going to write the request to SCOTUS?"

"It is my judgment that the prosecution should author it in keeping with legal procedure. Of course, the defense and the court will be given the opportunity to read and make suggestions before it is transmitted to the justices."

"Agreed," both sets of attorneys said.

"Then, court is adjourned."

"One thing, your Honor. It seems unfair that our client be forced to remain on Death Row for what is likely to prove to be a long, drawn-out process. We request that he be returned to the general population."

Judge Rotweillin did not take even half a minute of thought before rendering his ruling: "Denied," he said and banged his gavel.

The petition was written and agreed upon that very afternoon to ask the Court to order the lower court to send up the record of the case for their review. It was a good omen for the defense that the petition was assigned to Justice Marie Downey, the most liberal of the three members of the liberal group on the Court. She was also the most recent justice to be approved by the Senate. Things would have been preordained against McGee if the longest serving and by far the most conservative of the conservative wing had received the assignment. He was on record in another case where maladministration by the lower court resulted in a wrongful verdict.

He said, "[the petition called for] federal judicial intervention to overturn a state prisoner's conviction and sentence an "intrusion on state sovereignty … [that] over-rides the State's sovereign power to enforce societal norms through criminal law." That this was a federal case was possibly a different kettle of fish, but the defense firm and McGee were glad to be able to avoid one most difficult impediment to his freedom… and life.

Justice Downey accepted the urgency of the case with alacrity, and the clock began to tick.

PI Alice Mary Craig reported her conversation with Elmer Gorton to her employers and to the rest of the defense group working to free McGee. She included Mr. Gorton's willingness to testify even at risk to himself and his family.

A pessimist by experience, Stephen Blackwell pointed out the obvious, "It is pretty thin. May be hearsay; so, we have got to find and interview every person on shift the night in question, even if we have to get subpoenas. I don't need to remind any of you that we need people to testify in open court, or we have no chance of getting any of this into the record. Let's all concentrate on this as of now and catch them mostly unawares.

You know full well that all conversations have to be recorded, and every interviewee must be questioned separately. They must be kept separate from each other. Go ahead and book separate rooms in several different hotels to keep them apart until we have written and signed depositions. Keep it formal, and make it apparent that this is serious, so serious that the ones with the best info will have to testify. Promise WITSEC as a last recourse."

Caitlin visited the management of the 443 Park Avenue South Condominiums building and obtained the names, addresses, emails, and mobile numbers, of every staff person in the building when the altercation took place. Ivory made a courtesy visit to the main CMZ corporate offices to inform that the depositions were going to take place and that releasing of that information would constitute obstruction of justice.

Alice Mary and her two associates delivered the subpoenas to the none-too-pleased recipients. Two were downright balky and refused to cooperate.

"Why?" Alice Mary asked.

"You know perfectly why. This is a Teamster matter and directly involves the Mafia. I wouldn't survive a day, if I testified."

"You can enter WITSEC with a guarantee of protection."

"Look, I'm undocumented. That won't apply for me," both of them said.

"Not true. I will personally guarantee your safety," Alice Mary said, even though she was not at all sure she was on good legal ground.

"Okay, if you say so. I want it in writing."

Five other staff members wanted the same thing even though they were citizens.

There was a surprise in store for the interrogators. With the promises of safety all but one agreed to divulge what he or she had seen and heard and would be willing to testify. They did not like the fact that their work place was a mob facility. Only three of them had children; and fewer than half were married, which decreased the amount of trouble facing the interrogators and the defense team when trial rolled around.

The questions and answers were very similar since the incident was so clearly etched into the minds and memories of everyone who had been present.

Q: Tell me in your own words what took place in the lobby of the 443 Park Avenue South Condominiums building that evening.

A: It was a quiet night, nothing going on but getting the routine work done. Everybody recognized the fancy woman from the penthouse, Ms. Toussaint. She came in with this fat, thuggy looking dude. He had a pock-marked face with what looked like an old knife scar on his left cheek. He was dressed in a good fitting expensive suit—like from Brookes Brothers. They had obviously been arguing before they entered the lobby. She was crying, and his face was grim and frowny—gritting his teeth. He said something nasty to her,.. Do I have to say it?

Q: I'm afraid so. This is about a murder investigation; we can't be too dainty about things here.

A: Well, if I have to. He called her a whore and the B word. Said she had been unfaithful to one of the C soldiers. That guy was dead meat, he said. He asked her why she cheated on him, humiliated him.

Q: What did he mean by that, did he say?

A: He said she had told guys he had ED and even Viagra didn't work for him. She said she had other friends without such shaming problems. He roared and snarled, is they only way I can describe what he was trying to say. Then, he gave her a very hard back hand with his right. Hit her on the side of the neck and cold-cocked her. She was out on the floor, nose bleeding, and she had a big bruise growing on the side of her neck and on her lower jaw. I thought he might have killed the girl.

Q: What happened next?

A: The guy looked like a maniac. His face was purple; he was slobbering, trying to curse, but nothing sensible came out. I never saw anyone that angry before. Scared me. Finally, he got better hold of himself. He ordered us around like he owned the place. Told us all that he would kill us if any of this ever got out. I, for one, believed every word the mafia guy said.

Q: Then, what?

A: He ordered us to get her up to her suite and to keep mum about it all. We did what he said, and right… darn… quick about it. We dumped her on her bed and left her be. I avoided him and the other mafia guys like the plague after that.

Q: Let me get this straight. Was she alive when you left her there?"

A: Yeah, she woke up crying and moaning about the pain. She asked for an ice pack. We fixed her up as best we could. She asked—just like the fat thug did—for us not to say a thing about this. She said she was afraid the guy would kill her, and she was scared. We felt sorry for her, but there wasn't anything we could do."

Q: What about calling or going to the police?"

A: You're kidding, right? Think I have a death wish? Get real!

The team reported the findings and summarized: The thug–who was recognized by several staff members as Otto "Six-Fingers" Castellammarese, number two in the New York Genovese Family–was violent and committed both assault and battery along with verbal abuse against the well-known penthouse guest Madeleine Noémie Toussaint. That incident happened two weeks before Ms. Toussaint was found dead from a savage attack. Out of fear, all the witnesses remained silent and lied to detectives when questioned. At the moment—however–it looked as if the staff members were all willing to testify.

Blackwell took possession of the recordings and reported to the detectives who were still in charge of the police case, Lt. Daniel Eberhardt and Sgt. Emily Conraad. He had copies of the recordings and affidavits made and gave them to the detectives and kept the originals in his office safe.

Daniel thanked Mr. Blackwell and told him, "Looks like we have a new case going here. I hate this. It'll be like poking a wounded tiger. But, I guess that's why we get the big bucks, right?"

"Better you than me, Lieutenant. Please let me know how things go."

CHAPTER TWENTY-ONE

THE FRUIT OF THE PER SE DINNER WITH THE DEVILS

McGee twiddled his fingers in his Death Row Cell. The McGee Associates, the Blackwell investigative team, and most of the Detective Bureau of the NYPD, wrung their hands over what to do next. It was apparently up to the lead detectives Emily and Daniel. Their alternatives included a soft approach to the Teamsters and to the Mafia to serve subpoenas for depositions, or to launch a frontal SWAT attack and take down the two armies and bring them to One PP for questioning, or to ignore the evidence and let sleeping dogs lie, which would create a much unwanted firestorm in the media.

Events dictated than none of those options was going to prove to be necessary. Because the Genovese gambling syndicate crossed state lines, the FBI assumed jurisdiction over his case which was in the early stages of proving worth the effort they expended. When the NYPD detectives first arrested him in flagrante delicto—in the very act, as it were—he knew his life as a free man was over… unless. It took Carmine only a matter of minutes to make the decision to be a rat and to bargain for the best deal he could get. The NYPD detectives started with the man—Tony "The Nose" Pappalardo, who Carmine knew as a bouncer, and to whom he had paid little attention. However, he did order The Nose to put a hit on one of the Lucchese rival gamblers, and Carmine watched him torture the man for information before executing him. That information led to Pappalardo turning states evidence against the Teamsters Local 560. Union City, New Jersey, which helped the UCPD to solve two murders and to recruit four new CIs.

When the FBI were brought in, everything Carmine did or said was treated as a major secret. The Nose informed the special agents in the New York office that Carmine had bought and paid for juror number eight in the McGee case. Carmine readily agreed to testify that what Tony had said was the truth. The agents passed that information on to the US Attorney's Office.

As a result of the FBI's investigations, the three top Genovese capos went down, and with them the entire Bronx gambling, prostitution, and rackets business. The Luccheses filled the vacuum and felt a certain sort of warped gratitude to the NY coppers and the fibbies. Neither law enforcement agency was at all surprised at that turn of events—it was just work for another day in the eternal battle. The information harvest was considerable, and all the cops saw that as a real plus.

Special Agent Dwight Cranston took over as the lead in extracting every scrap of information possible from Carmine before the hood was released into WITSEC.

Q: Tell me a little story about Otto "Six-Fingers", Carmine. It has to be something we can verify.

A: That's what I signed the agreement for, and I keep my word. I seen Six Fingers with my own eyes, cut up that Toussaint broad. I helped hold her down. She was a real fighter, and Six Fingers couldn't do it hisself.

Q: How did he kill her?

A: Machete. Turned her into hamburger. [Pause for brief laughter on the part of the interviewee].

Q: How come there were no fingerprints or DNA from either one of you guys in the penthouse?

A: We called up Tony, The Nose; and he come up to the room and helped in the clean up where it counted. He has a rep as bein' the best cleaner.

Q: But there was one fingerprint on the machete. It belonged to someone else. How do you explain that?

A: Easy-peasy, we do it alla the time. We got a guy who does perfect work... name's Owen Langston. [pause for laughter] He teaches classes for the NYPD and your fibbie bunch. He even got a medal. I seen him stick a pointer fingerprint on the handle. The cops fell for it hook, line, and sinker. Some citizen went down for the whole bit—the "big bitch" [death sentence] for it. Poor smuck, but can't be helped, ya know.

Damien Markee steered the Luccheses in how to let the NYPD and the FBI do a world of hurt to the Genoveses. He knew the Luccheses had an inside guy, a made man, with the rival gang, and—for a price, of course—the guy, Niccolo diSalva Campania, was able to give Damien the last necessary piece of the puzzle surrounding McGee's trial, conviction, and grim sentence:

Q: Nicci, you told the boss you have some good intel on the Lythgoe snuffs. He wants the details because they will help get rid of the vermin [Lucchese colloquialism for the Genoveses] and build our empire. He promises you can come out from undercover and be a capo in Manhattan.

A: My memory says some money's gonna change hands, too. A 110 K bones, my memory tells me.

Q: I have a satchel with me right now. If your info is right, it's yours today.

A: Good, then, here's how it went down. The Don give the okay to Six Fingers to take out the Teamster boss Lythgoe and his wife. Six had to put up a coupla hunnert K for all the bother Don had to go to, see. Ya get nothin' for nothin'. Anyways, Six got a uptown cabinet maker to build him a box that looked just like a old timey camera. It had room for a baretta and a trigger that looked like a button to take a picture. Real clever thing. He give a bribe to the house-keeper to leave a birthday package in Mrs. Lythogoe's apartment—a gift guaranteed to go over with a bang [pause for raucous laughter]. Rocco Vanzetti looks more like a spic than a guinea; so, Fingers took him on to con some tourist from Podunk, Midwest to "take Lythogoe's last picture" [another pause for a good laugh]. Youse know that Lythgoe raped Six's granddaughter, Damien. When, Six heard about how it all went down, he threw a big party at Sanducci's Grill for the guys. Never seen a guy so pleased with hisself.

Q: One last question, Nicci, how did Otto "Six-Fingers" Castellammarese come up with the moniker, "Six-Fingers"? Do you know?

A: Yeah, that's a funny one. It's on accounta he has such big hands, it's like he has extra fingers. He always says 'it's better for holdin' a machete.'

The information—including the agreements for the informers to become testifiers and rich men of leisure—went quickly from Damien to Ivory to SA Cranston and to Deputy US Attorney Caruthers with the speed of light.

SCOTUS GETS THE
ANTEPENULTIMATE WORD

Justice Marie Downey, joined by Justices Stephanie Brinkman-Porter, and Helen Craghower, issued a scathing denial of the newest McGee certiorari. She described the previous decisions by Justice Clarence Baden-Leahy designed to prevent SCOTUS from acting to rescue prison inmates sent to prison with significantly flawed trial records [majority opinions written by Justice Baden-Leahy] as "perverse" and "illogical," writing that it "eviscerates" controlling case precedent and "mischaracterizes" other decisions of the Court. "The Court," she wrote, "arrogates power from Congress, improperly reconfigures the balance Congress struck in the [habeas amendments] between state interests and individual constitutional rights," and "gives short shrift to the egregious breakdowns of the adversarial system that occurred in these cases, breakdowns of the type that federal habeas review exists to correct."

As examples she cited the Baxter Broadhead certiorari which alleged that Broadhead's state court lawyers had failed to investigate available evidence that he was innocent. Broadhead continues to languish in prison. In the present case, that of US v. McGee, she reserved her most strenuous criticism: "Had the same justice been assigned the McGee case, in all likelihood, the present litigant would have met the same fate, but this time, at the peril of his life. The evidence for a new federal court trial in this matter is extremely compelling, and the Court hereby directs that a new trial inclusive of the potentially exculpatory evidence be commenced forthwith. The request for a writ of certiorari is hereby denied.

A litigant who loses in a federal court of appeals, or in the highest court of a state, may file a petition for a "writ of certiorari," which is a document asking the Supreme Court to review the case. In practical terms, denial returns the case to the original lower court for disposition. Customarily, the denial of the writ is simple and terse, without explanation. In the McGee case, Justice Downey's ire was up; and–to her way of thinking—it was time posthumous that justice was done, and the finicky legalistic reasons to deny justice by hardcore "law and order" justices was dealt with positively, hence the inclusion of the order from the Court.

The effect of Justice Downey's denial and in essence ordering a new trial in view of new evidence was stunning if not unprecedented. No one in New York or in the federal justice system was inclined to argue that the Court should change its ruling. It was beyond both the scope and interest provoked by the case. Judge Rotweillin scheduled the new trial for three weeks hence, even though his schedule would barely permit it. He was almost certain that it would be record short trial.

Both the prosecution and the defense agreed with his estimation, and each prepared carefully crafted plans to get their message out without incurring the judge's wrath or compromising the defendant or the government's position. Judge Rotweillin called for a pre-trial conference which excluded McGee himself.

"Ladies and Gentlemen, we are about to hold a hearing or trial, if you will, that will be as brief—I hope—as it is unusual. Let me hear from you about your opinions and something about how you will proceed. Mr. Caruthers, you first."

The Deputy US Attorney spoke from his chair, "Your Honor, we have been given verifiable exculpatory evidence in the McGee case, complete with witnesses, although a bit unsavory in several instances. A great deal of effort is afoot: the government is in the process of placing the witnesses in secure facilities and having the Marshalls prepare Witness Protection for them post trial. I believe we can be done with all of that by the date you scheduled. At that time, we will declare that charges be dismissed without prejudice."

"Mr. Blackwell."

"The defense concurs, but we ask that your Honor, and the prosecution agree to our calling several witnesses in the service of justice and the greater good. The witnesses we call will officially, under oath, and on record, admit to crimes they have committed and for which they have been immunized which will incriminate significant crime figures and others for felonies. We beg your permission, your Honor.

"Mr. Caruthers, do you agree?"

"Heartily, your Honor."

"Then, I order that the trial follow as you have described. Adjourned."

The issues of insulating and protecting the witnesses in what was rapidly becoming a major mafia trial required serious measures on the federal level. As a result, an entire section of Army Post Fort George G. Meade, Maryland, home to the Defense Information School, the Defense Media Activity, the United States Army Field Band, and the headquarters of United States Cyber Command, the National Security Agency, the Defense Courier Service, Defense Information Systems Agency headquarters, and the U.S. Navy's Cryptologic Warfare Group Six was cordoned off.

Hidden among those buildings is a specially designated, specially guarded and secure housing facility for immediately endangered people, especially those witnesses and their families involved in gang related trials where violence is expected. The area was isolated with double security for the witnesses during the McGee trial. Fort Meade is one of the most secure locations in the world—comparable to Fort Knox. The witnesses were well-aware of the danger they were in, and there was only minor grumbling heard from them.

The second issue was securing WITSEC Protection for those who qualified. Unusual haste was required to cut through the tedious red tape usually thrown up for applicants. The United States Attorney's Office for the District of Columbia is in charge of WITSEC/The Witness Security Program/WPP and The United States Federal Witness Protection Program also known as the Witness Security Program or WITSEC.

The WITSEC program was formally established under Title V of the Organized Crime Control Act of 1970, which in turn sets out the manner in which the United States Attorney General may provide for the relocation and protection of a witness or potential witness of the federal or state government in an official proceeding concerning organized crime or other serious offenses.

Fort George G. Meade is a major provider, particularly for armed physical security. As of 2020, approximately 19,000 witnesses and family members have been protected by the US Marshals Service since the program began.

No one in law enforcement had illusions about the criminality or scoff-law character of WITSEC protectees: 95% are—in fact—criminals. Nonetheless, the Attorney General is empowered to distribute $150 million in grants over five years for programs nationwide that would protect witnesses. The funding is currently available for over five years for programs nationwide that would protect witnesses in violent felony cases including homicides, serious drug offenses, and gang-related crimes. The authorization also provides matching grants to protect the witnesses, relocate them, and guarantee safe passage to court. The U.S. Marshals Service provides 24-hour protection to all witnesses while they are in a high-threat environment, including trials and other court appearances. Witnesses and their families typically get new identities with documentation.

The program is entirely voluntary. Witnesses are permitted to leave the program and return to their original identities at any time, although this is strongly discouraged by administrators and rarely occurs. In both criminal and civil matters involving protected witnesses, the US Marshals cooperate fully with local law enforcement and court authorities to bring witnesses to justice or to have them fulfill their legal responsibilities. The program is voluntary, but once entered, fulfilling the duties of a witness is not.

The level of fear and caution remained high during the pre-trial and brief trial period. As near as anyone could tell, the Genoveses were totally unaware that the trial was scheduled or that witness preparation and protection was in crisis mode. Even spies within the family were certain that the Genoveses knew nothing about what was coming at them. Nothing hinted of links to the press or anyone else from the defense, the prosecution, the judge's chambers, the witnesses themselves, any governmental agency—local, state, or federal—or certainly from the Luccheses. They were not in the habit of talking to their archrivals, the Genoveses. The secret appeared to be a completely locked up one.

Judge Rotweillin banged the gavel to open the trial. Despite the unrevealed plans for conduct of the trial, voir dire had been carried out and a jury empaneled. The jurors were more carefully screened and vetted than any previous panel in the history of the SDNY. The judge sequestered the 12 jurors and two alternates in several different hotels for sleeping and meals and scheduled a secure conference room in the archives area of the Museum of Modern Art for their deliberations, should any be required.

"As per usual, we will hear from the prosecution first," he said.

Deputy US Attorney General Franklin Caruthers began his combination prosecution presentation/evidence production/and summation speech:

"Ladies and Gentlemen of the jury. With the permission of his Honor, Judge Hyman Rotweillin, and the esteemed US attorneys general, we will have the defense present their witnesses first, then we will have an announcement."

His demeanor was stiff, proper, and unrevealing.

"Granted. Mr. Blackwell, call your first witness."

"The defense calls Number NYPD 10451-05222022 FEL-M,1."

He maintained a deadpan expression as the jury and those in the spectator seating began to whisper and murmur.

"Order in the court," Judge Rotweillin said and banged his gavel lightly.

Silence returned, and the entire population of the courtroom waited in anticipation for who or what "Number NYPD 10451-05222022 FEL-M,1" might be.

The courtroom main doors opened and two powerful guards in full combat gear marched into the room, each holding one of McGee's upper arms. McGee, himself, was dressed in blaze orange scrub suit with large black letters "DOC" on the back. He was in his customary wrist, waist, and ankle shackles. They marched him to the witness chair and stood behind him the entire time he was in the room. He was sworn in by the bailiff.

Q: Please state your name and place of residence, Sir, Blackwell said.

A: Joseph, Michael, Aloysius, John McGee, prison number 10451-05222022 FEL-M,1, SCU United States Federal Penitentiary, Terra Haute, Indiana.

Q: What do the letters "SCU" stand for?

A: Special Confinement Unit... Death Row."

Q: How long have you been confined there, Mr. McGee?

A: Two years, one month, thirteen days.

Q: What was the charge for which you were confined in the SCU?

A: Multiple first-degree murders.

Q: Are you guilty of those crimes, Sir?

Q: No, Sir.

It was McGee's turn to display a deadpan expression.

Q: How is it that you are here today to testify?

A: I was ordered to do so by Justice Marie Downey of the United States Supreme Court.

"Thank you, no further questions."

McGee was escorted out of the room the same way he came in, a Death Row Inmate.

"Next witness."

"The defense calls Carmine Giuffrida."

The gangster was dressed in a custom-made Brook's Brothers suit, charcoal grey with very fine purple pin stripes, a light lavender silk shirt, and matching tie, pointed toed tan shoes, obviously new.

Blackwell ran through the usual questions and got the routine answers. Then, he got to the point.

Q: Where is your current residence located?

A: I respectfully refuse to answer because I am ordered not to do so by The United States Attorney's Office for the District of Columbia.

Q: Are you a registrant in the Witness Security Program, otherwise known as WITSEC?

A: I respectfully…

Q: Have you been given immunity for your past crimes, Sir?

A: Yeah

Q: What were those crimes?

A; He gave a litany from his RAP sheet, and admitted there in open court that he was given immunity for three murders, one more murder as an accomplice, for participation in racketeering, RICO offenses, drug, and gun, distribution.

Q: Do you know a person named Otto "Six-Fingers" Castellammarese?

A: Yeah.

Q: What is your relationship with him?

A: He's the underboss in the Genoveses. I am a caporegime under him, and I take his orders and do some of his wet work.

Q: For the record, what is wet work?

A: Murder and torture.

Q: Can you give us examples with details of person, time, and place?

A: Sure. Carmine went on for ten minutes to describe in ghastly detail the torture murder of Madeleine Noémie Toussaint. He admitted to having beaten the woman into submission and defenseless; so, the underboss could take out his volcanic anger and hack the once attractive woman to a slow death. He included the placement of bogus finger-prints from McGee—one of Six-finger's main enemies—on the handle of the machete his boss used. He described in detail how he cleaned up every place in the apartment where Six-finger's prints or DNA could possibly be.

Q: And you are admitting to being an accomplice to Ms. Toussaint's murder, Mr. Giuffrida?

A: Yeah, I am. I'm a gang big shot; it's what I do.

Q: Let's change subjects. Mr. Giuffrida, what can you tell us about the murders of Henry Kendall Lythgoe, President of Local Union No. 295 International Brotherhood of Teamsters, his wife, Mary Margaret O'L. Lythgoe, and their unborn child?

A: First off, let me say that Lythgoe wasn't no saint. He knew where all the bodies was buried, like Jimmie Hoffa's for example. He was mobbed up all the way. A big shot with the Genoveses.

Guiffrida went on to describe all the preparations for Lythgoes' murders, including the manufacture of the fake antique camera and the placement of the excellent index fingerprint from McGee inside the camera box, and the recruitment of the innocent tourist, Gladys Owens Perkins, from Kansas City, Kansas, to be the dupe who everyone saw pull the trigger.

Q: One last question, Mr. Giuffrida. Please describe in detail exactly how the fingerprints of a man called McGee were obtained, duplicated, and placed into the camera box.

A: That one wasn't so easy, but I took care a it like I usually did for Six-fingers.

Q: Pardon me for interrupting, but, is it your testimony that Otto "Six-Fingers" Castellammarese gave you orders to murder the Lythgoes and specifically to obtain McGee's prints and to plant them?

A: Yeah, that's just what I was sayin'. Now let me finish. This here's the interestin' part. He gave exact dates and times for meeting with Romano Vespasianu in his lower Manhattan backroom where the man created nearly infallible fake passports, driver licenses, certificates of graduation, etc., and fingerprints. Giuffrida described the sophisticated instruments Romano used–the cell phone sized FP201 and FP202 devices–biometric Android terminals which integrate a performant IDEMIA biometric optical sensor to capture fingerprints accurately for many legal business purposes.

However, for the nefarious purposes of Carmine and Otto, perfect fingerprint transfers were one of the specialties of Romano, for which he was well paid. Carmine observed the actual transfer of McGee's fingerprints to the camera box and the machete, a process he described in comprehensive exhaustive detail. It was spellbinding and convincing to the jury.

"No further questions for this witness. The prosecution rests."

"Anything from the defense, Mr. Caruthers?"

"No, your honor, the defense rests."

"I promised that this trial would be brief. We have adequate time, are you ready with your summations, Counselors?"

"We are, your Honor," both attorneys said, almost as if they had scripted the wording and timing of the responses.

"Proceed, Mr. Caruthers."

"In light of this new and overwhelmingly convincing evidence, the prosecution withdraws its assertion of guilt on the part of JPAMJ McGee and requests that your Honor vacate the previous verdict and replace it with a judgment of not guilty."

"Defense?"

"No objections. We are in full agreement with the prosecutor."

"Then, it is the judgment of this court that new evidence introduced in this courtroom today requires a finding of not guilty on all charges and issues an apology for Mr. McGee having endured difficulties in the course of finding justice. The jury is dismissed with gratitude for their patient service. However, each of you has sworn an oath of silence on what has transpired her today, and you are still bound by that oath until the conclusion of a Grand Jury, which will be sworn in today. I trust you recognize the duty you owe to the court, to the safety of Mr. McGee and all potential witnesses, and to the very cause of justice. Court is adjourned."

He banged his gavel with enthusiasm.

The Grand Jury in the matter of US v. Castellammarese, Vespasianu, D'Arco, & Markee, et al, convened two months later. Witnesses, testimony, and verdicts, were kept secret as were most outcomes, in the interest of security and justice. The NYPD and FBI gained three new paid Confidential Informants; D'Arco and Castellammarese maintained their Genovese positions, and Elmer Gorton was elected to be the new General President of the International Brotherhood of Teamsters. 41 True Bills of Indictment were served. Markee was no-billed.

McGee received a letter from President Norcroft-Daniels and took a vacation in the Bahamas for a month. His two partners accepted only high priority cases in the interim.

–THE END–